California
Connection 3

California
Connection 3

Chunichi

www.urbanbooks.net

Urban Books, LLC
78 East Industry Court
Deer Park, NY 11729

ISBN 13: 978-1-60162-504-5
ISBN 10: 1-60162-504-9

First Printing December 2011
Printed in the United States of America

10 9 8 7 6 5 4 3 2 1

Distributed by Kensington Publishing Corp.
Submit Wholesale Orders to:
Kensington Publishing Corp.
C/O Penguin Group (USA) Inc.
Attention: Order Processing
405 Murray Hill Parkway
East Rutherford, NJ 07073-2316
Phone: 1-800-526-0275
Fax: 1-800-227-9604

Chapter 1

Jewel

"Snitch Bitch"

"Baby, how much longer before you get here?" I asked Touch in my sweetest voice.

"About fifteen minutes," he replied then hung up.

There was a lump in my throat as big as a rock hanging up the phone. I swallowed in an attempt to get it down. With my head hung low, I gently rubbed my stomach and thought about my unborn child.

"Take your positions, guys. He'll be here shortly!" the head detective instructed his guys to man their posts to prepare for Touch's arrival.

"Please forgive Mommy, baby," I whispered toward my protruding stomach. "I just want the best for you."

My palms started to sweat, my heart was racing, and tears rolled down my eyes. Seconds seemed like minutes, and minutes seemed like hours, as I waited for Touch to come home. I knew as soon as he walked through the door they would sweep him away and I would never see him again. My child would be without a father, and I would lose the love of my life. But I also knew with life comes sacrifices, and this was just a sacrifice I had to make. It was either him or me, and there was no way I was gonna give birth to my child in jail.

"You sure you got this?" the police officer asked me as he escorted me from my bedroom to the living room.

"Yes, officer!" I rolled my eyes, sick of the officers constantly checking to make sure I was down for this.

"You just stay hidden in the bedroom—"

"Oh my God!" I yelled, interrupting the officer mid-sentence. "We've been over this too many times." He'd gone over the instructions time and time again. I had it already!

"Just want to make sure you're not having any second thoughts or planning to try anything tricky. If this goes wrong, it's your head, little lady."

Save your threats, asshole; they don't scare me, I thought. I definitely wasn't having second thoughts. At this point it was all about my baby. The only thing I had to worry about was getting the fuck out of dodge when this was all over with because I knew, once Touch realized I was the bitch who got this show in motion, all hell would break loose.

"He's here," I heard another police officer announce from the hallway.

I looked out the window to see Touch cautiously walking up to the house. Now I was having second thoughts. The fifteen minutes came sooner than I expected.

The officer quickly whisked me into the bedroom. My nerves were building, and it took all I had to refrain from bursting into tears.

"Honey, I'm home," Touched yelled as he opened the front door, a huge smile across his face.

Within seconds cops came out from every closet, corner, and room in my house, commands coming from every direction as they rushed Touch with weapons pulled.

"Don't move!

"Freeze!"

"Hands in the air!"

Touch was surrounded. Taken by surprise, and with no chance to run and nowhere to escape, he stood frozen. Despite all the warning the cops gave me, I couldn't resist looking out into the living room. All eyes were on him, but his eyes were only fixated on me. There was a cold look in his eyes. A look I'd never seen before. I could imagine it was a look of disgust, hurt, anger, and betrayal. Maybe that's why I'd never seen this look before because I'd never done such a thing to him to warrant such emotions.

Touch yelled out, "How the fuck could you do this to me? After all we've been through, Jewel! You bitch!"

I felt ashamed that I had set him up. I had to keep telling myself it was for my own good, the good of my unborn baby.

With my cover blown, the officers didn't try and stop me when I walked out of the bedroom. They moved him to the kitchen, and I watched as Touch placed his hands on the counter and the officers patted him down. For a second, I thought I saw a tear in his eyes. Unable to bear the pain, I turned away.

"Answer me!" Touch demanded. "Answer me!"

I refused to give him any explanation. Besides, I knew it would only anger him even more.

"It's over, Touch. Say good-bye," one of the officers said.

Suddenly, in one cat-like movement, Touch reached in the kitchen drawer, pulled out a small handgun, and *Pow!*

An enormous force slammed into me, and I fell to my feet as a stinging pain ripped through my stomach. I looked down to see my white shirt soaked with bright red blood.

"Oh my God!" I screamed out in a panic. "He shot me! He shot me!"

My body jolted, and I shot straight up. I was panting and sweating. I was confused as I looked around the quiet room. *Where is the police? Where is Touch?*

I rubbed my eyes and gathered myself. It was then I realized I was still in bed. I'd been dreaming. I breathed a huge sigh of relief as I gathered myself. *Whew!* Why was I having this dream? The vividness of it scared the shit out of me. What did it mean?

Chapter 2

Touch

"One-way Ticket to Jail"

The minute I heard I was wanted for conspiracy I disappeared. I didn't even bother telling Jewel I was getting ghost, I just vanished. Well, not really vanished. I went and holed up at my other girl, Lisa's house. We never went out together, and I never told any of my boys about her. She was my side bitch, and as long as I kept her lifestyle funded, she never complained.

It had been weeks since my disappearance, and I was really starting to miss Jewel. Not a day went by that I didn't think of her and my unborn child. I'd spent days wondering if it was a boy or a girl, and who it would look like, if it would look like my other kids, me, or Jewel.

I was excited about having a kid with Jewel because I knew I would always have access to it. Unlike with my other kids. Their mother was a bitch who never let me see my babies, and it hurt. I wanted the best for all my babies, but this new one was going to get spoiled. I already knew that.

I wondered if Jewel was eating right. I was hoping she was seeing the doctor and taking care of herself. Sometimes I even wondered if the stress of all the bullshit would cause her to have a miscarriage.

Life was truly fucked up, and I had no idea I'd be so miserable without Jewel and my unborn child. Being on the run was for the fucking birds!

When I'd unexpectedly caught conspiracy charges, Lisa was my only hope. I had no place else to hole up. I damn sure wasn't about to go to one of my boys' houses. Those loose-lipped niggas would have told someone where I was laying my head. And a hotel was out of the question because I wasn't about to pay some crazy amount of money to get caught on video surveillance cameras. So I had been laying low at Lisa's crib until I could figure out my next move.

"Have you seen my Ben and Jerry's mint chocolate chip ice cream?" Lisa asked me, a look of disgust on her face.

Lisa had just come home from work. She hadn't been in the house five damn minutes, and she was already tripping. Lisa was cool with being my side chick, but lately she was really starting to annoy a nigga. I don't know what her problem was, but it seemed that since my money had run low, her attitude was all out of whack. I guess my pops was right when he warned me, "Women think you ain't shit when your paper ain't right. But as long as you got money, they respect you."

"Yeah, I ate it a couple of hours ago," I responded, trying my best to keep my focus on ESPN.

"Well, can you go run to the store and pick me up some more? I've had a long day at work, and I was really looking forward to coming home and eating my ice cream," she expressed with some attitude.

This bitch must be on dope. Is she forgetting I am wanted? I looked at Lisa like she was a damn fool. I didn't know if it was that time of the month for her or what, but she was really on some shit lately.

I rarely went out the house, and if I did go out, I was dressed in all black, with dark shades, and a fucking rastaman hat with fake dreads. I wasn't about to go through all that for some ice cream! I wanted to cuss Lisa's ass out for talking stupid, but I stayed calm in an attempt to keep the peace. I needed her crib to stay and only had about two hundred dollars to my name.

I tried to smooth things over. "When my paper gets right, I will pick up anything you want, baby girl."

Lisa snapped at me, "Go do something! Get a job! Because I'm tired of you laying around here."

I already had enough on my plate, so dealing with a nagging woman every day wasn't something I needed. Waiting for the perfect time to make a move wasn't easy. It took patience and planning, because one wrong move could easily get a nigga locked up. I was miserable not being able to move around the way I used to.

With the word on the street that I was wanted, nobody was willing to fuck with me on no business shit. I had no connects. I knew in a time like this I needed to be with Jewel. She was a true rider. She would have found a way to make shit right. Lisa, on the other hand, was selfish as hell and stingy with her money and her pussy.

"You know damn well I can't go get no fuckin' job! So, for once, will you just shut the fuck up with your smart-ass comments? I'm trying to watch the game." I turned the volume up on the TV.

"Nigga, please! I pay the cable bill in this house." Lisa grabbed the remote out of my hand and turned the TV off. "If I have something to say, you damn sure are going to listen." She then threw the remote back at me.

That was the last straw. This bitch had been riding my ass for the past week. I couldn't take it anymore. That move sent me into a rage. I grabbed Lisa by the neck and slammed her on the couch. I'd lost it for a minute. It wasn't until I noticed blood all over her face that I snapped back to reality.

When it was all said and done, I'd choked her and punched her in the face, giving her a bloody nose. Realizing I'd truly fucked up, I quickly let her go. I just couldn't control my rage sometimes. I had one domestic abuse case on my hands, and I sure as shit wasn't looking for another.

"You done fucked up, muthafucka," Lisa screamed and ran to the kitchen. She grabbed a knife and started after me.

I picked up Lisa's car keys and ran for the garage. My time with her was up. Time to find a new place to crash.

"Get the hell out of my house! And if you take my car, your ass is going to jail," she shouted as I rushed into the garage and jumped in her car.

I knew what she was saying was probably true, but at the time, I was all out of options. I pressed the garage opener and threw the car in reverse.

Lisa banged on the hood of the car as I was backing out the driveway.

Boom! Boom! Boom!

"Your ass is going to jail!" she shouted. "Stupid-ass nigga!"

I put the car in drive and sped off, leaving her standing in the middle of the street. I looked in my rearview mirror and saw her on her cell phone. I already knew what that meant. That bitch was calling the police. I needed to get rid of her car fast.

I had no idea where to go. I didn't want to involve Jewel in any more of my bullshit, so her crib was off limits. It seemed my only hope was Lexi, my baby mother. She and I had ended on a real fucked-up note—with a domestic abuse rap. In fact, I couldn't stand the bitch, but I had no other choice, so I headed her way.

After twenty minutes of cruising down the highway, constantly looking over my shoulder and making sure to abide by the speed limit, I was at my baby mother's exit. Two more minutes and I would be at her crib. I couldn't believe I had made it all the way here.

I was hoping Lexi would let me in. My plan was to drop the car a few blocks away and walk the rest of the distance to her house. That didn't happen because, as soon as I exited the ramp, blue lights were flashing from every direction.

"Muthafucka!" I yelled to no one in particular.

I wondered how the fuck they had found me. *No use trying to figure that shit out now.* I needed to figure a way out. My first instinct was to jump out the car and run, but my out-of-shape ass wouldn't have made it one block, so I pulled over. My plan was to talk my way out of this predicament.

The cop came to the window and asked for my driver's license and registration. I grabbed the registration from the glove box then began to search for my ID. *Damn!* I realized I had no identification. I had purposely stopped carrying it on me since I was wanted. I had planned on getting me a fake ID but kept putting it off. Now I was really fucked up.

It didn't take long for the cop to slam me against the car and arrest me for driving a stolen vehicle, and assault and battery. *This is some real bullshit,* I thought as I was being hauled off to the city jail.

I'd only been in jail a week, but it seemed like a month. I knew once I got processed and they realized I had those conspiracy charges, there would be no bond in my future. Because of jail overcrowding I sat in a holding cell for an entire week. This was my first day on the block, and I was looking forward to finally having an opportunity to use the phone. I stood in line patiently. It was taking forever, so I kept my mouth shut, not wanting to start any trouble.

The dude in front of me finally got off the phone. I had a feeling he wasn't even talking to anyone, that he was just being a dick and holding up the line on purpose.

The first person I thought to call was Jewel, who'd been on my mind all week. Hell, just the previous night, I beat off my dick, thinking about her sexy body and phat ass. I wasted no time dialing Jewel up. I hadn't really spoken to her since I'd disappeared. There were a few three-second conversations where I told her I was alive and safe, but that was it. I was paranoid her phone was being tapped, so I would always cut it short.

"Touch? Baby?" Jewel yelled into the phone, after accepting the collect call.

Before I had a chance to respond, I felt a shove in my back.

"Get off the phone," this dude demanded.

"Fuck you mean, nigga? I been waiting for the phone for an hour. Get yo' ass in line, duke!" I said, pointing toward the end of the line.

Bop!

I took a punch to the stomach. Obviously this man wasn't up for conversation. But I wasn't no punk, so I gave him a fight like he wanted.

Bam! I hit him in the head with the phone receiver.

Immediately he and I were throwing blows at each other.

"Yo', yo', yo'!" I heard someone yell. "Back up off him," the voice calmly said.

The dude I was fighting released his grip and backed up off me. I watched as he skulked away like a dog with its tail between his legs. I looked up to see an old head standing over me. He reached out his hand and helped me off the ground.

"Thanks, man," I said as I brushed my clothes off.

The man walked me over to a nearby cell. "Clear this bunk," he ordered another dude sitting in the cell. The dude immediately got up and left the cell. It didn't take me long for me to figure out this old head ran things in the block and all these niggas was scared of him.

"Son, we need to talk," he said to me.

"A'ight." I agreed right away. There was no way I was gonna challenge this cat.

"You all right, Touch?" he asked.

"I'll make it. How do you know my name?"

"I know everything about the streets. I heard you were doing some big things, until you caught those drug charges. You kinda remind me of myself when I was your age. My name is Jimmy. Tell me your story, youngblood."

"Nice to meet you, Jimmy. Thanks for stepping in back there, although I coulda handled that dude myself."

"I know, young'un, I know."

"You wanna know my story? A'ight. I been hustling since I was in grade school. My father was a hustler. He left my moms when I was a baby, but he was always around the neighborhood, so I saw him a lot. His daddy was a hustler, and he brought all three of his sons into the game. My pops and his two brothers ran the streets for a while there. Then the cops decided they was enemy number one and shot my dad and arrested my uncles, Mike and Kendall."

"I know those two cats. They doing a bid in the federal pen, right?"

"Yeah, that's them. Damn! That's crazy. How you know those two?"

"We used to run together on the streets. How you think I know about you?"

"I like that. You a smooth nigga."

"Young buck, don't you ever call me that again. I ain't no nigga, you hear? That's the trouble with you young fools today, calling each other nigga this, nigga that."

"Word. I apologize. You right."

"Continue."

"Well, after my pops passed, I figured it was time for me to man up. I started hustling on the streets. It was small at first, but because people respected my old man, I got a lot of help, and my business started to grow. People were paying attention. Including the cops. I was careful, so I operated for years without getting one bust. Then I got a domestic abuse charge on me, and that's when the cops really started gunning for me. They had some big old undercover sting to set my ass up. Now I'm looking at some conspiracy charges."

"Son, you got heart just like your daddy. You and me can do some big things, but you got to keep your nose clean though. You willing to listen and learn?"

"Hell yeah, my nig—yes, sir."

Jimmy smirked and nodded slowly. He patted me on my shoulder and walked out of the cell. From that point on, he took me under his wing. He even made plans to put me on to some work when I got out. Things were looking up. Now I needed to take care of all these bullshit charges against me.

Chapter 3

Jewel

"Free My Man"

It had been days since my brief phone call from Touch, so I took it upon myself to call Virginia Beach City Jail and find out their visiting schedule. I wasn't able to make it until the weekend, so Touch was going to have to wait another few days before he could get a look at me.

I made sure I looked my best as I straightened my hair and applied my makeup. I squeezed my plump booty into my tightest pair of jeans, sure to show every crease and curve. I hadn't seen my prince in nearly three months, so I wanted to put a smile on his face.

When I reached the jail, I went through visitor check-in and was in the back visiting with Touch in no time. It was much quicker than the two-hour waits I had endured during my visits to Norfolk City Jail. I barely had time to even start the book I had brought along to read before I was called into the visitors' room.

"Hey, baby!" I yelled and waved as soon as I saw Touch walking up to our designated glass booth.

It was a bitter-sweet moment. While it was great to see him, it was sad to see him under such circumstances. His hair was freshly braided as though he'd just left the shop, and his smile was still gleaming white and perfect. Besides the orange jumpsuit, he was the same Touch I'd always known. He actually might have been a little bit more muscular from the weights he had been lifting.

"What's up, baby girl?" Touch said through the phone receiver.

"I miss you so much. You look good." I said, admiring my man and touching the glass that separated us.

"Thanks. You look good too. You got my dick rising." Touch massaged his penis as he spoke. "It don't even look like you have gained a pound. Are you eating okay? You making sure my son, a'ight?"

"Oh, I'm good. Let's not worry about me. The question is, Are you okay in there? Do you need anything? What exactly are your charges, and how did you get caught anyway?" I spat one question after another.

"Damn! Jewel. Hold up. I feel like I'm under interrogation." Touch gave me that million-dollar smile then added, "The important thing is, I'm no longer on the run, and I got a bond. The bond is one hundred thousand dollars. I need you to holla at the bondsman and give him ten grand."

There was an instant lump in my throat and a pit in my stomach. *Ten thousand dollars? Where the hell am I gonna get that?* I thought as I listened to Touch's instructions.

Touch must have noticed the worried look on my face. "What's the problem, Jewel? Why you looking all crazy and shit?"

"Well, baby, it's just that I don't have that kind of money." I cringed as I explained, knowing Touch wasn't going to be happy. I was now happy there was a barrier between us.

Touch yelled, "What you mean, Jewel? I left fifty thousand dollars behind when I left the house."

"Touch, it's been three months! We have a mortgage, two car notes, and a shitload of credit card bills." I kept my tone even, but I was pissed. He left me high and dry. What did he expect?

"So you mean to tell me you blew fifty grand in three months? You don't even have ten Gs to get a nigga out?" Touch shook his head then dropped his head down into his hand.

Seeing him look so defeated made me feel real fucked up inside. I had to make things right. "Don't you worry, baby. I got this. You will be out by morning. You know I've never let you down before, and I'm not about to start now."

"Now that's the Jewel I know." Touch smiled, his mood instantly brightening.

The brief tension between us subsided. We talked away. About how he was faring in there, about how his meeting this old head named Jimmy. The whole time I just wanted to touch him and kiss him. Before we knew it, our visiting time was up. We tried to prolong our good-byes as long as possible, but the damn COs were being assholes.

"Love you, baby. *Mwah!*" I kissed him through the phone. I was getting emotional but tried to stay strong for my man. It was no use. I couldn't stop the tears.

"Love you too. Take care of my baby boy." Touch then hung up the phone.

I watched his back as he walked away and the heavy steel door slammed behind him.

"Damn it!" I yelled after jumping back into the truck.

I didn't know how I was going to get ten thousand dollars by the next morning. Touch's fifty thousand had dwindled down to a mere four thousand dollars. I knew if I didn't get him out by the time morning hit, they might find out about his conspiracy charges. Then he may never get out. I stayed calm as I thought of my options.

After a few minutes of thinking, I made a phone call. A call I didn't really want to make. *I hope this shit works*, I thought after dialing a phone number on my cell.

"'S up?" Rico said after answering the phone.

Rico was a little side item I'd had for the past few months. Before Touch was on the run, we were having problems and had decided to split up. He was seeing other chicks, so after a while, I decided to date too. And that's where Rico came in. Rico was a nice guy. He worked as an engineer for the United States government. He had dough, and the best thing about it was that it was legit. I usually liked my men a little rough around the edges, but after the shit I'd gone through with Touch, it was time for a change. He was everything opposite of Touch.

"Hey, baby. How are you?" I asked.

"I'm still tired from the ride you gave two nights ago. Other than that, I'm good. What's going on with you?"

"Well, I've some great news." I tried to sound excited.

"Oh, yeah? What's that? You're coming over to ride me again?" Rico asked playfully.

"I got accepted into nursing school, and I start next week." I lied.

"Damn, baby! Congratulations!" Rico said, happy about the news. "You ain't even tell a nigga you had applied for school. I'll tell you what. Let me buy your books for you. It will be my present to you."

That shit was easier than I thought. Little did Rico know, I was prepared to beg, fuck, suck, and do something strange for a little change, but to my surprise, I didn't even have to ask. This nigga offered, so I wasted no time going in for the kill.

"Oh my God! Are you serious?"

"Come on, baby girl. You know I'm big on education. I'm proud to see you trying to do something for yourself. I got you."

"Well, I need about seven thousand to cover everything," I said in a whiny voice.

"No problem. You're worth every penny. Plus, after you finish school, a shitload of money will be rolling in. Come over and get it when you're ready."

"I'm on my way." I breathed a sigh of relief.

I started my truck and headed to Rico's house. As soon as I walked in, he had the money waiting for me. Of course, after giving me the money, he wanted to celebrate my acceptance to nursing school by dicking me down. Normally I loved sex with Rico, but this time I wasn't interested in him touching me at all. My mind was on Touch and getting back with him.

"Baby, I can't," I said between kisses.

"What's wrong? It's that time of the month?"

My initial thought was to agree and tell Rico I was on my cycle, but the one huge lie I'd just told him was enough. My conscience wouldn't allow me to tell another.

"No, honey. I've got some business I need to take care of, and I've gotta do it right away." I gently rubbed Rico's erect dick.

I was about to rain-check his ass and dip out the door, but seeing the look on his face and afraid he would take the money back, I got on my knees and gave him some head. It didn't take him long to nut all over the place. I zipped his pants back up, gave him a small kiss on the cheek, then headed out the door, leaving him drooling at the mouth.

When I got back into my truck, I whipped out my cell phone and called Touch's lawyer. I informed him I had the money for bond and made an appointment for them to discuss his options. Next, I called up a bail bondsman well known to all the guys into the drug game. In fact this bondsman used to be a drug dealer himself, except he was one of those smart enough to turn his drug money into something legit. Sad to say, but even I had to use his services once.

I felt proud as I met the bondsman at the jail. I had exceeded Touch's expectation. I got the money, talked to the lawyer, and got his ass that same night.

I waited patiently for Touch to walk from behind the jail walls. As soon as I saw him, I rushed toward him and jumped into his arms.

"What's up, baby girl?" Touch said as I kissed him all over his face.

"Looks like your dick," I responded, rubbing on his erect penis.

"Yeah, that's all for you tonight." Touch laughed, and we hopped in the car.

The ride seemed like it took forever. All I wanted to do was get home, get naked, and ride Touch all night long. I asked him how he had gotten caught, and he was pretty vague. I felt like he wasn't telling me everything. I wasn't going to push it, because I was just so happy to see him again.

Touch smacked my ass before we entered the house. "You didn't give my pussy away, did you?"

"You know this pussy is yours." I assured him with a kiss.

I was dressed in a trench coat. Touch didn't think anything of it because there was a chilly nip in the air. Underneath my trench coat I wore a skimpy French maid set with a small apron to match. My five-inch stilettos added an extra touch. As soon as we entered through the front door, I dropped my coat.

"Damn, Jewel! You never cease to surprise a nigga. I love that about you." Touch hugged me close.

I could have sworn within seconds his dick grew at least two inches. And it got even harder as I began stroking it.

After Touch stripped right in front of me, I quickly got on my knees and started deep-throating his dick.

He pulled my head in even closer. "Aah, man. Don't stop."

I knew just what it took to send him to the moon. My head was definitely like no other. The key with Touch wasn't my tongue, it was the way I stroked his dick. I could make him come in less than five minutes. But I made sure not to give him too much because I wanted him to last all night.

Touch ripped my lingerie off and carried me up the stairs into the bedroom through the gardenia petals lightly covering the foyer floor and trailing up the stairs leading to the bedroom. My pussy instantly became wet. After he let me down, I pulled him onto the bed. I began massaging him, working my way down to his feet. After his massage I turned on the surround sound CD player. Jeremih's song, "Birthday Sex" started to play. Touch's birthday was a few days away, so this was an early present. I began dancing to the song.

Touch loved to see me feel all over myself. Popping my pussy in front of him was his favorite. Not being able to take the uprising sexual tension, he grabbed me up and lifted me up against the wall.

"Which titty do you want in my mouth while I fuck you?" he asked, sticking his thick penis inside of me.

"The right."

For the next hour we had sex in every position thinkable. He literally put me to sleep that night.

For the next few days, Touch didn't leave my side. Besides having sex, all he wanted to do was rub my stomach. After a while, it became quite annoying. He was truly about the birth of his baby. He was convinced it was a boy. I, on the other hand, wasn't so sure.

Meanwhile, Rico was blowing up my phone. He'd been texting and calling me continuously. At first I was playing it off like I was in class and couldn't return his calls or texts. But that didn't work for long. All he did was start calling and texting at night. I was doing everything, from sneaking to the bathroom to text him to making bullshit trips to the store to call him. I was afraid it was becoming too obvious that something was up, and the last thing I wanted was Touch to catch on to what I was doing. I turned my phone on silent and ignored all Rico's calls and texts. Pretty soon I began getting calls from strange numbers and private numbers, but I was on to that trick. I knew it was Rico. He was doing anything he could to get me to answer.

Finally I could no longer ignore it. I figured if I just answered one time Rico would stop calling. I snuck upstairs while Touch was sleeping, so I could answer Rico's call.

"Hello?" I said in a soft tone, trying not to make too much noise.

"Hey, sweetie. Where have you been? I've been calling you for days?" Rico said before giving me a chance to respond. "I'm right in front of your house. I was just about to knock on the door when you answered."

"Oh my God! Rico, no!" I panicked. I felt as though I was gonna shit in my Victoria's Secret G-string. "I'm not home yet. I'm on my way, but I need to stop at the store."

With Touch's temper, if Rico had come knocking, there was gonna be a fight, possibly a death, and it sure wouldn't have been Touch doing the dying.

"Okay, I'll wait for you here."

"No, I'm gonna be a little while. Meet me at the grocery store." I started getting my outfit together.

On my way to the garage I peeped in on Touch to make sure he was still asleep. Luckily I hadn't awaken him, and he was sleeping like a baby. I grabbed my keys off the kitchen counter. From the living room I looked out the window and watched as Rico got in his car and pulled off. I rushed in my car and headed out my neighborhood in the opposite direction.

I met Rico at the store. He'd beat me to the store, since I took the long way from my house.

"Hey, baby. What's going on?" Rico said as soon as I got out my car.

I planned on going the distance with this lie and walking around the grocery store and shopping, hoping to bore Rico into leaving while I shopped for my house. But as soon as I saw his face, I changed my tactic.

I told him, "Listen, baby, you can't come over. This is not a good idea."

"What are you talking about?"

I took a deep breath in. I really liked Rico, so it wasn't easy for me to tell him. "My man is back home." I let out the breath I had taken in and prepared myself for his verbal onslaught.

From the day I'd met Rico, I had told him about Touch. Sure, I should have done things a little different and maybe prepared him for this day, but it all happened so quickly. I was hoping he would just go away on his own, but he didn't. So I decided to just put it out there to keep him from getting killed.

"So that's how it is, Jewel? And to think I really was feeling you. You didn't even respect me enough to let me know what was going on. This is how I had to find out? Cool." Rico simply walked away, got in his car, and pulled off.

Damn! That hurt me more than if he had gone off on me. At that point I didn't know what to think. I expected and would have accepted name-calling or the standard "Fuck you!" but a dude talking calm, no cursing or anything, now that was strange. It unnerved me a little bit.

All sorts of thoughts began to run through my brain. *Could this linger into something else? Do I need to tell Touch so he can protect himself? Hell, do I need to carry a gun to protect myself?* I didn't know if Rico was crazy or what. I'd just taken seven grand from this dude then dissed him. I figured it wouldn't be long before he put two and two together and realized I'd used his money to bond Touch.

As soon as I walked in the house through the garage door, Touch was standing in the kitchen waiting on me. "Where did you go?" he asked after biting into a turkey sandwich.

"To the store," I said, startled.

"So what you buy?"

"Oh, I didn't get anything because they didn't have what I was looking for," I said, unable to come up with anything better.

"It must have been important because you left in a hurry. What were you looking for?" Touch wasn't letting up so easy.

"Huh? What you mean?" I said, trying to buy time to come up with an answer to satisfy Touch and get him off my ass.

"What was it that you were looking for at the store that you couldn't find?" Touch repeated, like he was talking to a child.

"Oh, I was just craving for some white Oreos. You know, pregnancy craving." I knew anything about the baby would ease Touch's mind.

"Oh, okay." Touch gulped down a glass of juice and headed out the kitchen. "For a second I thought you had run off to see a little dude around the corner or something." He chuckled. "Don't let me find out," he said as he playfully smacked my ass.

I knew he wasn't joking though. If he found out I had gone to see another dude, there would be hell to pay.

"Yeah, your brother." I played along, relieved he hadn't caught me in my lie.

Throughout the evening the private calls continued back to back. I had to wonder what sane person would spend hours constantly calling a person's phone. Rico was really starting to scare me.

Later that night, Touch and I went to the store to pick up a few things. The whole time while shopping I couldn't help this overwhelming feeling that someone was watching us. Especially as we put our groceries in the truck.

I scanned the parking lot but didn't see anyone. I looked in the large windows of the grocery store, and everyone inside looked suspicious to me. I didn't know if it was paranoia or what, but I was wishing I had a gun at that moment. It freaked me out to the point where I considered telling Touch about Rico.

Just as Touch started the engine and put the truck into gear, someone knocked on the driver's side window. The knock was so startling, I screamed out loud and jumped in my seat.

"Touch, don't open the window," I warned and pleaded at the same time.

Touch looked at me like I was losing it. "The fuck you talking about?" He pressed the button, and the window rolled down. "Damn, dude! You scared the shit outta me and my girl," he said to the man standing there.

"Oh, I'm sorry. It's just that you dropped this before you closed the trunk." The man held up a box of white Oreos."

"Oh, damn! Good lookin', my man. My girl would have been sad not have these at home. She's carrying my son, and she got those cravings." Touch was smiling as he took the Oreo's and handed them to me.

"No worries." The man walked away toward the store.

My heart was racing. I had thought for sure the knock was Rico about to blast away. I didn't know what to do then. I couldn't keep living on edge like this. I had a big decision to make—tell Touch or handle Rico myself.

Chapter 4

Lisa

"Prank Calling"

"Fuck you, Touch!" I screamed as I slammed the picture frame against the corner of the counter, shattering the glass.

I took out the picture of us and ripped it over and over again until it was in tiny little pieces. Tears streamed from my eyes. I couldn't believe this nigga used me for a place to stay, for my money, and for my pussy. I really thought he genuinely cared about me. I'd had his back from day one then he had the nerve to put his fucking hands on me! For a minute I actually felt bad for calling the police on him, but the more I thought about it, the more I realized he deserved to get some time for what he had done to me.

After he flipped out on me I was determined to teach him a lesson. Yes, I called the cops on his sorry ass, but I wasn't finished there. I wasn't going to be satisfied with the cops arresting his ass. He needed to be punished by me personally. His personal life needed some fucking with. Little did he know, I'd been calling his bitch girlfriend, Jewel, whose number I'd gotten from his phone when he was staying with me. I knew the day would come when I could use it.

Ring! Ring! Ring! I called Jewel, expecting the phone to ring out to voice mail like it usually did. I had been calling her over and over again, basically harassing that bitch. I never left a message, I just wanted to annoy her. I hadn't fully thought about what I wanted to do yet. I was just playing some childish games with her at this point. I have to admit it took me back to junior high school when I prank-called people. That was kind of fun.

To my surprise, she answered.

"Hello."

I was taken off guard. I didn't say a word. I quickly pressed the mute button on my television so there was no background noise. Couldn't let her try and get any clues as to who it could be.

"*Hell-fuckin'-o!*" Jewel yelled into the phone.

Although I wanted to say something to her so bad, I continued to remain silent.

"If I ever fuckin' find out who this is, I'm gonna choke the fuckin' life out of you! Stop calling my got-damn phone!"

I could feel the fury, yet it was so comical. It was working, I was unnerving this little bitch.

To avoid bursting out in laughter, I hung up the phone. I guess the average chick would call me a scary bitch because I never said anything, but that's the beauty of it all. That bitch had no idea it was me ringing her phone, which was definitely some fun-ass shit.

As the day passed, I continued to call Jewel's phone, but she never answered again. For a while all I was getting was her voice mail right away. I guess my constant calling had forced her to turn her phone off.

Bored with the calling, I decided to take things to the next level. I logged on to my computer and did a reverse search using Jewel's cell number, but nothing came up. Then I tried Touch. Still nothing. I needed more information if I was going to take this harassment to the next level.

"Think, Lisa, think," I said aloud to myself as I wracked my brain. "The car registration!" I rushed to the kitchen and grabbed Touch's keys. The dumb ass had taken my car. Guess he wasn't smart enough to realize I would call and report my car stolen.

His car had been in my garage since he was on the run. He'd refused to drive it because he knew that was a sure ticket to jail. I pressed the key and unlocked the doors to his car. I looked in the glove compartment and saw the registration. It was registered to an out-of-state address, but at least I had his full name. I rushed back to the computer. This time I did a search using his full name and date of birth.

"Bingo!" I shouted as his information came up. I'd hit the jackpot.

I paid a $29.95 Internet detective fee. It was well worth it. It listed all of his previous addresses as well as relatives. I was even able to get Jewel's information because it had her listed as a spouse. I leaned back in my chair, pleased with my progress. I felt like one smart bitch. With that said, I decided to call it a night.

On my way upstairs I decided to give Jewel one last call. "Here we go again." I yawned then dialed Jewel's number.

"Hello."

Like last time, I said nothing as I sat on the edge of my bed.

"Hello," she said for the second time.

Again, I remained silent and lay back on my bed. Then I heard Jewel say, "Touch, come listen to this shit, so you hear it for yourself."

"Hello?"

Touch was now on the phone. My nerves went straight to my stomach when I heard him. I didn't say a word, but it took all I had.

"I'm muthafuckin' sick of this nonsense," Jewel shouted from the background. "This person has nothing better to do but play silly-ass games on the phone."

"Yo'! Who the fuck is this?" Touch yelled in the phone, damn near bursting my eardrum.

I couldn't handle it anymore. Hearing his voice made me lose my composure. "Your worst nightmare, muthafucka!" I said quickly then hung up the phone.

The plan was for me to keep my identity a mystery, but when I heard Touch's voice, I couldn't remain silent. I turned my lights off and got in the bed. I couldn't sleep as I continuously replayed in my head what had just happened. I was too worked up. My nerves and adrenaline were working overtime.

Wow! Touch is home and didn't even bother to call me. I couldn't believe it. I knew he was probably upset with me about the whole stolen car and domestic violence thing, but I had thought he would at least call and try to apologize. Even if he wasn't sorry, I thought he would try to kiss my ass so that I'd drop the charges. Guess I was wrong about that. The more I thought about things, the angrier I got.

I quickly dialed Touch's phone after I blocked my phone number from his caller ID. He didn't answer, and I was sent to voice mail. After twenty attempts, I eventually gave up and headed to sleep.

As I drifted off to sleep, I thought, *Touch just can't come in and out of people life as he pleases. He would be so upset if Jewel loses that sweet little baby of his. Tomorrow, I'll be sure to leave her a little gift on the doorstep. Vengeance is best served shaken up and cold. Touch will pay for what he's done to me.*

Chapter 5

Touch

"A Liar's Lie"

"You ready?" I asked Jewel as she was slipping into a black minidress.

This dress was one of my favorites. It fit every curve of her body perfectly. I watched as she tugged on her dress, making sure everything was in the right spot. My dick rose as I lusted over her perfect body. I noticed Jewel's ass was the same size, but her titties seemed to be two sizes bigger. But the strangest thing was, her stomach was flat as a board.

"Damn, baby! Is my baby boy growing at all?" I questioned. I knew Jewel was only a few months pregnant, but I at least expected her to have a little pudge or something.

"Touch, everybody doesn't get big right away. Some women don't even start showing until five months." Jewel then walked into the bathroom, and I followed behind her.

"Well, have you at least been going to your prenatal visits and stuff?" I was concerned that something might be wrong with my baby. I would never forgive myself if something happened and we didn't do everything we could to prevent it.

"Touch, please! You're driving me nuts!" she shouted, obviously frustrated. "Go watch TV or something. I'll be ready in a few."

Not wanting to have a rocky start to the day, I backed off and did as Jewel asked. As I sat in the living room watching TV, I kept thinking about how happy I was about my child-to-be. I just knew it was a boy. As I came out of my daydream, I noticed the time.

"Jewel, hurry up!" I shouted.

"Give me ten minutes," she yelled back. "I'm almost done."

We were on our way to pay my lawyer a visit, and if Jewel didn't hurry, we were gonna be late. Mr. Schultz was all about his business, and time was money. This dude actually charged extra for each minute you were late. I didn't blame him. With the clients he had, he needed to be a ball-buster. I'd been dealing with him since the start of my criminal career, but that made no difference to him. This man didn't deal with credit, good faith, or give a fuck about all the other times I'd paid him up front. Times are now, and he wanted his money right now. I couldn't argue with him. He was good at what he did, and I respected his game.

"Jewel!" I yelled out to her again.

She shouted back, "Trayvon Davis, leave me alone!"

What the hell she could be doing that was taking so damn long? For a minute I wondered if she was stalling on purpose. It wouldn't be the first time she would have done it.

Jewel always hated going to see the lawyer. What she feared the most was the unknown; not knowing how much time I may or may not get was probably driving her crazy. I admit I had put my baby through a lot. Every woman has a limit. I had to wonder if I had pushed Jewel over hers. I constantly thought about blowing the trial and just copping a plea, but my rap sheet was fifteen years strong. There's no telling how long the D.A. would want to put me away. I couldn't take that chance. I'd rather take my chances with a sympathetic jury and let the chips fall where they may. *Damn! This wasn't how I imagined my life would turn out. I was supposed to be living on some private island by now.*

I got tired of waiting and even more tired of thinking about court and all my problems. I headed to our bedroom to drag Jewel out. As I approached the bathroom door, I could hear her talking.

"I'll call you back." She hung up the phone just as I was walking in the bathroom.

"Oh, that's what's taking you so long. Who was that?" I was a little heated but tried to stay calm.

"One of my girls."

Now I was suspicious. "Girls? You ain't got no girls."

"You don't know what I have," Jewel snapped. "You've been ghost for over three months, remember?"

"A'ight, Jewel. Let's roll," I said, still trying to avoid an argument. She was right. I had disappeared, but now I was ready to make it up. For Jewel and my baby.

"Okay. I'm ready," she replied with a fake smile going through the motions.

Jewel seemed a bit on edge all morning. At first I just figured it was because of our upcoming visit with the lawyer, but the more I observed her, it seemed like it was something more. I started tripping, thinking it had to do with her pregnancy and that the phone call earlier was to her doctor.

I started feeling guilty on our ride over to the lawyer, thinking Jewel deserved way better than this. The funny thing is, I think she had realized it faster than me. But that's life. I learned a long time ago the sun will still rise whether you stand alone or with someone by your side. That's why my loyalty was always to the almighty dollar and the streets. They came before anyone and anything in my life. Now I was starting to rethink that motto. Jewel was breaking down that code.

As we drove, Jewel's phone was constantly buzzing. It was seriously starting to bug my ass. I couldn't even enjoy the tunes on my mixed CD because of it.

"Damn, Jewel! Who the fuck keeps calling?" I asked, annoyed as hell.

"It's that same person that's been calling private. I have answered the phone a thousand times with nobody talking on the other end. You know how it goes, Touch."

"They still calling? Why don't you just change your number, babe?"

"I thought about it, but so many important people have this number, and so many things are going on right now, I just really don't think it's a good idea."

Although I felt what Jewel was saying was a bunch of bullshit and the person calling was whoever she was talking with earlier, I didn't even bother saying anything. I didn't have the energy to fight with her at the moment. I was trying to get rid of the drama between the two of us, so instead of slapping the bitch for lying to me, I just turned up the volume and let the music take me into a deep zone.

As I bobbed my head to the words of "6 Foot 7 Foot" by Lil Wayne, my moment of attempted meditation was interrupted by Jewel's constant texting. Now my patience was starting to run thin with her, and I felt like I was gonna explode.

Without hesitation, I snatched Jewel's phone from her hand and started going through her call log and text messages. Jewel had been acting real suspicious lately, and I couldn't ignore it anymore. I knew she had been sneaking to the garage and various places throughout the house to use her phone while she thought I was sleeping. There was no doubt in my mind Jewel was hiding something, and I was about to find out what it was.

I read the text in her phone aloud—"I haven't heard from you. Call me. You did some real fucked-up shit. Jewel, I know you're not in school. You're a fuckin' liar. I would have given you anything."

"Okay, you happy? Now please give me the phone back, Touch," she said, trying her best to stay cool.

"Jewel, who the fuck is Rico?"

"Oh, you want to go there?" Jewel said in a sarcastic tone.

"I'ma ask you one more time—Who the fuck is Rico?" I had her in a semi-choke hold, causing her to almost hit the person in front of us.

"Get your fuckin' hands off me," she struggled to say, but I wasn't letting up until she answered my question. She pulled the car to the side of the road, and within seconds she somehow pulled out a taser gun.

"What the fuck is this?" I laughed as I released her.

"Now, nigga, *you* listen to me. You fucked up our relationship a long time ago. Then you were on the run while I was alone and pregnant. On top of that, your sorry ass is up for domestic violence charges for another bitch! So, please, I beg you, don't come at me with a whole bunch of questions!"

Damn! I thought as I listened to Jewel. There was nothing I could say in response to that. Everything she said was true. Her words rendered me silent. The only good response would have been to apologize, but there was no way in hell I would have done that at that moment.

"Oh, you quiet now, huh? You don't have shit to say." Jewel put the car in park.

"Nope. No time to talk right now. We'll talk later. We got more important things to take care of," I said, blowing off the conversation then stepping out the car.

"Fuck you, Touch! Go handle your business by your fuckin' self. You've done this plenty of times before. You know the routine." Jewel then drove off.

I didn't have the time or energy to chase after her. I just shook my head in disbelief and began walking to my lawyer's building. Everything seemed to be spiraling out of my control, and I had no idea what to do about it. I wanted to make everything easy for Jewel, but sometimes I got the feeling she didn't want me around. Nothing I did was right.

Fuck it! I thought. *I'll just do me from now on.*

I somehow reached Schultz's building on time. I pressed number eight on the elevator and walked in the office. As I sat waiting to see Mr. Schultz, I thought,

What bullshit is this? He would make me pay extra for being late, but when I was on time, he made me wait and wouldn't give me no damn discount. That's the price I had to pay for having the best attorney in town. I'd rather pay his ass than do time.

The receptionist said, "Mr. Schultz can see you now."

"Thanks," I said while walking toward his office.

"Mr. Davis." Schultz greeted me with a handshake.

"Thanks for taking me at such short notice. Here's your money. It's all hundreds, just the way you prefer." I bit my tongue and didn't say nothing about the double standard.

"You know me well." Mr. Schultz accepted the money and motioned for me to have a seat. "Listen, let's get to it because I don't want to take too much of your time. I've already talked with the district attorney."

"Wow! That was fast. That's why I fuck with you, Mr. Schultz!"

"Yeah, I took her out last night, so I figured I may as well discuss the case while I had her eating out of the palm of my hand. Everything in life is about who you know and how much power they hold. From church to the law, it's all politics, my friend."

"I know all about. I'm just glad to have you in my corner."

"Money talks!" Schultz laughed. "The conspiracy charges will be dropped due to the lack of evidence. As you may already know, the police officer working undercover on your case died in the line of duty. She was involved in a tragic high-speed chase." Schultz cut his eyes at me. He knew it was me she was chasing. He took a sip of his coffee. "The prosecutors hoped to still be able to go on with the case, based on the reports from the officer. But the files from the case have mysteriously disappeared." Schultz cut his eyes at me again.

Now I knew nothing about the missing files. I damn sure was glad to hear the news though.

"As far as the domestic violence and the auto theft charges, you will have a hefty fine, be required to go to anger management class, and unsupervised probation for a year. So I need you to stay on your best behavior at all times. No fighting, smoking, drinking, or drugs. And if you decide to do it, don't fuckin' get caught. You got it?"

"Damn right!" I said. This was the best news I could have possibly heard. Way better than I'd expected.

"This time, you got real lucky. Your court date is in two weeks. I will have my receptionist send you a reminder in the mail."

"I'll be there. Thanks, man! I'll see you in court," I replied, happy as hell.

I walked out of the office with a big-ass Kool-Aid smile across my face. To my surprise, Jewel was waiting for me in the parking lot with the tazer gun still in her hand. Believe it or not, not even that was able to ruin my joy. With her being pregnant, I knew her hormones were all fucked up.

I gave her a hug. "Thanks for coming back for me."

She looked shocked as hell. She didn't know how to respond to my friendly attitude. She just got in the car and started it up. I had just gotten the best news in my life and didn't want to ruin the moment. I just wanted to go home, smoke a blunt, and lay down. I know Schultz told me to stay away from drugs and alcohol, but I had been up the last two nights awaiting my fate, stressed as a motherfucker. For the first time in months I was stress free! I needed a rest.

The entire ride home, Jewel and I didn't say a word to each other. She didn't even ask about what happened with my lawyer. I didn't know if it was because she was scared to hear or if she didn't care. Either way, that was cool with me. I was finally able to listen to my CD and zone out without interruption. I blasted the radio, leaned my seat back and turned up the tunes of "I'm on One" by DJ Khaled. I sang along.

When we arrived home, Jewel didn't even pull in the driveway. She dropped me off and pulled right back off. I didn't even question it. There was no way she was going to ruin my good mood. I walked right on to the crib and didn't even look back. I figured she was acting out because she wanted a reaction from me. And, more than anything, she wanted an explanation and an apology. True, she deserved it, but I wasn't quite ready to give in yet. She would get what she wanted but on my terms.

When I got in the house, I did exactly as I'd planned. I rolled a blunt, grabbed the remote, and got comfortable in the bed. I hadn't taken two pulls from the blunt before my cell phone rang. I looked at the caller ID, but I didn't recognize the number. I wondered if it was that bitch Lisa, who had been blowing my phone up on the regular. It was time to put an end to this shit.

"Hello," I answered full of attitude, ready to let Lisa's ass have it.

"Yo', Touch, this is Jimmy. What's been going on?"

"Oh, damn! Jimmy, it's good to hear from you. I just left my lawyer's office, and shit is lovely right now. Those conspiracy charges are dropped. Somehow paperwork got fucked up."

"Like I told you when you were in here, it's all about who you know. You'll be surprised the things people will do for money."

"True, true." I wondered if Jimmy had anything to do with my good fortune. I wanted to ask him but knew that "the man" was probably listening in on the other end.

"I need you to check out something for me. My boy Deuce called you on three-way for me. He gon' call you back a little later." Jimmy abruptly hung up the phone.

Ten minutes later I got a call from Deuce, just like Jimmy said.

"Talk to me," I said after answering the phone.

"You a cocky muthafucka," the voice responded, laughing.

"Hey, what's going on?" I was hoping I didn't fuck myself by saying that.

"This is Deuce. I don't do too much talking on the phone. Meet me at Tiny's Bar. Can you make it there in thirty minutes?"

"Yes, I can."

No sooner than I hung up the phone with Deuce, I realized I didn't have a ride to meet him. Jewel hadn't returned home yet, and my car was still in Lisa's garage. I needed to get my shit back.

With no other choice, I called a cab. Fifteen minutes later, I heard a horn blow outside. My cab had arrived.

I hopped in the backseat. "Tiny's bar," I told the driver.

"You got it." The fat, greasy-haired, white dude put the car into drive.

As I was riding to meet Deuce, my thoughts turned back to my car and Lisa. *I can't believe this bitch has been calling Jewel's phone. How the fuck did she get her number? I've really gotten myself in a fucked-up situation.*

A side of me wanted to go to her house and fuck her up again, but another side of me thought, *Maybe I should bait her in.* After all, that bitch had my car, and if I gave her a little attention, said the right words, I could not only get my car back, I could probably convince her to drop the charges.

I had to clear my mind as we pulled up to the lounge where I was meeting Deuce. I paid the driver and hopped out the funky-smelling taxi. Homeboy needed a shower bad.

With two football games set to air that night, the bar was packed. I walked in, grabbed a seat, and ordered a bottle of Guinness. I sat thinking about the risk I was taking, dealing with Jimmy and his friend. I didn't really know these dudes at all. Yeah, Jimmy knew my pops, but what if they were actually enemies and he was setting me up to get revenge? Why was he so eager to help me in the joint? I decided I needed to be on guard while dealing with these dudes.

The fucked-up thing was, no matter how much doubt I had, I had no other choice than to fuck with Jimmy and Deuce. The word on the street was, I was on the run at one point and just got out of jail. When niggas hear shit like that, they scatter away like roaches when the light comes on. No one wants to be seen dealing with a wanted brother. Some real disloyal motherfuckers out here on the streets.

An older dude sat down next to me. "Touch."

"Deuce?" I replied, unsure if this was him.

"That I am. What's up, man?"

"Chilling."

We dapped each other up.

Deuce told the bartender, "Can I get two shots of vodka?"

Dressed in a grey sweatshirt, dingy jeans, sneakers and a Pittsburgh Steelers hat, Deuce smelled of oil, so I assumed his day job had to be working on cars. I could tell by his demeanor that he was old-school just like Jimmy.

"Jimmy must really like you, youngblood," Deuce said. "He doesn't usually take such risks."

"Risk?"

"You heard me right, son. If it was up to me alone, you wouldn't be in on the business. I don't need no youngblood fuckin' up my paper."

"Well, lucky for me, it ain't up to you," I spat, a little offended. "I'm gonna get mine, just like the next man. I don't want to mess with my paper or anyone else's."

Deuce didn't say anything after that. He just stared me straight in my eyes. I wasn't going to be intimidated by him, so I met his eyes with the same intensity. I knew I could probably take him if it came down to fists, so I challenged him with my eyes for him to make the first move.

Deuce ended our little game of chicken by saying, "Well, you have an opportunity to make some money. Are you in or out?" He broke eye contact and took a sip of his drink.

Without even knowing what I was agreeing to, I said, "I'm in."

Our handshake symbolized me signing my name on the dotted line of a contract.

"Well, you start tonight. Don't fuck it up," he informed me. "This is the deal—I'll give you the product, you get rid of it and bring back fifty percent of the profit. That goes to Jimmy."

"Just like that, huh?"

It was a hell of a deal, but I was a little leery. It was almost too good to be true, but I couldn't afford to say no. I needed the money, and Jimmy was the only one willing to deal with me.

"That's it. You keep the money coming, and I'll keep the product coming."

Then we made arrangements for me to pick up my first couple kilos of cocaine. I really didn't like working on consignment, but a nigga was broke and needed a start.

I left the bar feeling on top of the world. My case was dropped, and I got put on to a way to make some major cash. This was the best day I'd had in a long time. I hopped in the cab humming the tune of "It Was a Good Day" by Ice Cube.

Chapter 6

Jewel

"Baby Snatcher"

After dropping Touch off at the house, I barely gave him time to close the car door before I sped off. I wouldn't have minded running over his pinky toe in the process. Touch had truly pissed me off! True, I was guilty for not telling him about Rico, but he had the nerve to question me, when he'd been living with another chick! I needed a little relaxation, so I decided to make a last-minute spa appointment. Luckily, I was a loyal customer, and they fit me right in.

"May I help you?" the receptionist asked as soon as I walked in.

"Yes, I'm here for my for eleven o'clock appointment with Miriam," I responded.

POSH was an exclusive day spa with all the trimmings, and Miriam was my favorite. Not only was she a wonderful masseuse, but she was also a great esthetician. I'd planned to get the works. I'd requested a manicure, pedicure, a ninety-minute deep tissue massage, facial, and body wrap.

Although this was supposed to be a time of relaxation, I found myself spending a lot of time thinking
about Touch and all his mistakes and fuckups. In
the beginning we were a match made in heaven, best
friends turned lovers. He was everything I ever wanted
and needed in a man. But it seemed like the more
money he made, the more problems we had.

We ran into a little problem with the law, and things
went downhill from there. When Touch and I both got
caught in an undercover sting operation, it caused a
huge rift between us. He thought I would rat him out,
no matter how much I tried to calm him. I got taken by
surprise by the investigation as much as he did.

Luckily for me, the charges got dropped because my
attorney found a loophole in the law and convinced
the judge that the charges against me were illegal.
Good thing too. I don't think I would have been able to
handle jail. I liked the finer things in life, and prison at-
tire didn't suit my body. At times, I had begun to think
I may be falling out of love with Touch. A woman can
only take so much. R. Kelly had sent a warning to all
men with the song, "When a Woman's Fed Up." Well,
this woman was reaching that point, and fast.

"Jewel, now I'm gonna give you a little extra attention and really focus on your head and scalp massage,"
Miriam said as she let my hair down. "I noticed you're
very tense, so I wanted to see if we can release a little
tension you have in that area."

"Gladly." I nodded.

This kind of massage was the best part. One simple
massage stroke of my scalp started draining my stress,
my irritation, and my resentment of Touch. *That nigga
should be grateful I been in his corner for so long.*

As Miriam massaged my head with her magic touch, I was beginning to feel totally relaxed, so I closed my eyes. The first person I thought of was Rico. He'd always said that I deserved better out of life, but it was up to me to make it better. The more I thought about it, the more I realized he was right. I needed to make a change in my life. If I wanted the finer things, I needed to go out and get them. I couldn't rely on some street-ass nigga to provide for me.

Despite the fact I fucked Rico over, he still called from time to time and left messages saying he just wanted to hear my voice so he would know I was okay. He was a real gentleman, unlike most of the niggas I dealt with. I started regretting that I'd really fucked Rico over. A couple of times I had thought about calling him, but I was ashamed of the way I had treated him. I knew what I did was wrong.

Lying on the table, fully relaxed, I was considering calling and patching things up with him. Rico showed me nothing but kindness since the day we met. He was beginning to fall for me. I would be able to have the finer things if I went back to him. I began to compare Rico and Touch. *Rico is stable. Touch's sorry ass damn sure is not. I need stability, no drama, and less chaos. With Touch, I never know if he is really in my corner. The only thing he has been truly been loyal to is the streets. I have always come in second place, which is so unfair to me. Rico seems to be all about me.*

The more I thought about it, the more it became clear that Touch wasn't good for me. *So why do I keep going back to him? I think I might be afraid to let go of him.*

Four hours, later my time of relaxation was over, and it was time to head home.

My anxiety slowly started to rise as I pulled into the neighborhood. I took a deep breath and continuously recited the words, "I will not fight with Touch tonight."

While pulling up to the house, I noticed a box at the front door. Getting excited about the package, I parked in the driveway instead of pulling into the garage, since it would be easier for me to just pick up the package and go through the front door. I'd ordered some Victoria's Secret and was surprised it had arrived so soon. Receiving packages in the mail always improved my mood.

As I got closer to the box, I noticed it was already open. Feeling that someone had opened my package and stolen my lingerie, I began to get angry.

Damn, these grimy-ass niggas out here, I thought, approaching the box. I quickly grabbed it and glanced inside. "Oh my God!" I screamed and dropped the box in a panic. "It's a baby!"

Inside the box lay a baby with a knife in the heart. Without thinking, I quickly grabbed the baby from the box. I thought that maybe there was still a chance to save it.

The second I touched it, I realized it was a plastic doll. "What the fuck?" I yelled.

I was fuming inside, wondering who the fuck would do such a wicked act. The first thing that came to mind was one of Touch's psycho bitches.

I rushed inside the house with tears in my eyes. This was the final straw. I know Touch had fucked a lot of women even while he was with me, but this crossed the line. As soon as I opened the door, Touch was right there.

"Jewel, what's wrong, baby? I heard you yelling." He grabbed me in an attempt to console me.

"Don't touch me!" I yelled, pushing him away.

Touch yelled as he noticed the baby in my arms. "What the fuck is this?"

"What does it look like, Touch? It's a gift that someone left on our doorstep."

"What?

"Yeah. It's probably one of your psycho bitches you be fuckin'."

"Hell, nah. That bitch don't know where we live."

"Ha! Busted, you stupid moron! What specific bitch are you referring to?" I threw the doll at him.

"Damn! Chill, Jewel. I don't know who did this, Jewel."

"Touch, what is really going on with you and that chick you got that domestic charge from? I need to know what's going on. My life could be in danger." I tried explaining to Touch the seriousness of the situation.

"Don't overreact. There's nothing to worry about. I will find the muthafucka that did this and make them pay."

"Oh, really? How would you find this person? Do you have an idea who it is or something?"

Touch shook his head. "I said I don't know."

The thought that someone was bold enough to step foot on my doorstep and leave a bloody doll was crazy. This was way too over the top for me. I felt like I was having a nervous breakdown.

I quickly went into the kitchen and grabbed a bottle of wine with a glass and made my way down to the basement to unwind. "I need some time alone!" I yelled as I walked away without looking back. I didn't even want to look at Touch.

I filled the Jacuzzi up with hot water and bubbles, turned on Kelly Rowland, and filled my wineglass with Riesling. As I sat soaking in the tub, I started thinking about all of my enemies. *But who would be evil enough to do such a heinous thing?*

The first person that came to mind was Sasha, an old friend of mine. She'd done some real fucked-up things in the past, but it had been nearly a year since I'd heard from her. She had just disappeared, and no one knew where she had gone. But something told me it wasn't her.

Then my mind traveled to Rico. After all, I had lied to him and taken ten thousand dollars from him to bail out Touch. He did have a reason to be pissed at me. A small part of me wouldn't blame him for seeking revenge. Any thought I had of getting back with Rico was now out the window. I wondered if he had really flipped his lid. Honestly I had no idea what this man was capable of doing. It's always the quiet ones who are the most dangerous. For a minute I even contemplated telling Touch about Rico; it would only be fair to tell him. Our lives could be in danger.

I took the last sip of my Riesling, turned up my music, lay my head back on my bath pillow, and closed my eyes. I was totally relaxed as the tune of "Motivation" floated through my head. I moved my hand to my midsection as I listened to the words of Lil Wayne.

With each verse I massaged my clit in a circular motion, moving my hips in rhythm with the music. I could feel myself reaching my peak as I imagined sitting on Lil Wayne's face, gripping his dreads tight.

Minutes later, after I'd satisfied myself, a true feeling of total relaxation sent me into a doze.

"How could you do this?" a whisper interrupted my moment of euphoria.

"What did you say?" I looked around the room nervously. I could barely make out the person's voice.

"For the first time, in a long time, I actually wanted to treat a woman right, and here you come with the bullshit. Jewel, man, you broke my fuckin' heart."

A face finally appeared from a dark corner of the room.

"Rico, I—"

"I didn't fuckin' say you could speak," he said as he pressed the cold metal tip of a gun to my stomach. "I think we both can agree that you have done enough. Right now all your ass is going to do is listen, and when I'm done, I might let you speak."

I nodded my head to let him know I understood very well. My mind was racing, my heart was fluttering, and I was too terrified to move an inch. All I could do was pray Touch would come to my rescue. He was upstairs somewhere probably high and drunk, while this nigga Rico was trying to make this my last living night in the basement.

"This pain is unbearable. I thought you were the one for me. I have a few questions, and you damn sure better answer them," Rico said.

I nodded again, the gun still lodged into my stomach.

"Did you ever love me?" he questioned.

"Yes," I said without hesitation. I didn't love Rico, but I knew at this point it was either do or die. I had to say exactly what he wanted to hear in order to save my life.

"Oh, yeah. So, that dude upstairs, do you love him more than me?"

"Rico, why are you doing this?" I begged.

"Shut the fuck up, Jewel! I didn't say you could speak. Now answer me. Does Touch have more of a special place in your heart than me?"

"No," I said, trying to assure him he was the love of my life.

"Jewel, your ass ain't too convincing. I bet if I had a thousand dollars in my hand ready to give then you would put on a good show for me. You always were about the dollar. I was nothing but kind to you. I wanted to take care of you. All I wanted in return was you to love me and accept me," he stated, becoming angrier and angrier.

"Rico, baby, I do love you," I said as I caressed the side of his face.

"You lyin' bitch!" He smacked my hand away from his face. "Shit ain't gone ever change. You're nothing but a manipulative, gold-digging whore. It is what it is though. Now open wide for me," he demanded as he placed the gun in my mouth.

Pow! The trigger went off, jerking my head back into the wall.

I woke up to the sound of my wineglass shattering on the basement floor. I was in a cold sweat.

"Damn! Rico is haunting me in my dreams," I said to no one in particular.

I gathered myself, grabbed a towel, and got out the Jacuzzi, careful not to step in glass. I headed up the stairs feeling guilty as hell for playing with Rico's emotions.

Chapter 7

Touch

"Rude Awakening"

I answered the phone not knowing who it was. "Yeah."

Its constant buzzing had finally broken my sleep. My neck was stiff from sleeping on the couch, and my head was hurting from all the Hennessy I'd drunk the night before. My hangover was so bad, the entire room was blurry and spinning.

I figured if someone was calling so many times this early in the morning, it had to be important. I hated to be woken up out of my sleep, so I was in no mood for bullshit.

"Hey, boo," a female voice said from the other end of the phone.

I looked at the caller ID. I didn't recognize the number, but the voice sounded familiar. "Who the fuck is this?"

"You know who it is. It's the chick you beat the shit out of then stole her car. Anyway, what did you think of your baby girl? Wasn't she beautiful? She was even dressed in a Juicy Couture onesie with matching socks and hat. Wasn't that little outfit so cute? I would have had her delivered a few days earlier, but FedEx was a little backed up."

Lisa had the sweetest little tone to her voice, like she was shooting the shit with one of her girls. My blood was boiling as I listened to the words this bitch was saying to me.

"Lisa, if you ever muthafuckin' step foot on my property, I promise you, you won't leave this bitch walking."

"Now is that any way to talk to a woman that holds your freedom in her hands? That was a threat, Touch. Did you forget you've already been charged with domestic violence? Now a recorded threat like that was not a smart move, honey." Lisa laughed then hung up the phone.

Her taunting was driving me over the edge. Not only did she have my court date hanging over me, now she had a recording of me threatening her. I felt like I could drive over to that bitch house and choke the breath out of her ass that exact moment.

In no shape to do anything at the moment, I struggled to my feet and headed to the kitchen to grab a bottle of water out of the fridge. I noticed the baby doll on the kitchen counter, and as I walked past, I saw a piece of paper attached to the blanket it was wrapped in. It read: *When life comes, so does death. Time is precious. Take advantage of it while you can.*

I thought to myself, *This bitch is really trying to fuck with my mental. Well, at least now I know who been causing all this chaos. It shouldn't be much of a problem to put an end to this.*

The more I thought about Lisa and the stunts she was pulling, the angrier I got. She was playing me, and it pissed me off. I needed to figure out a way to put an end to her games.

"Stupid bitch! Do she know who the fuck I am? I will kill that bitch." I snatched the doll from the kitchen counter and took it to the trashcan. As I came back from the garage, I met Jewel.

"Why are you yelling at this time of the morning, Touch?" she asked, tying her silk robe together.

"Sorry, bae. I didn't mean to wake you up. Go back to sleep. I just had a little too much to drink. Let's go back to bed." I didn't want to tell Jewel about the call I'd received from Lisa or that Lisa was the culprit behind all the prank calls.

I walked with Jewel to the bedroom and hopped in bed beside her.

"I love you," I whispered in her ear while holding her tight. "And Daddy loves you too, Junior," I said, rubbing her belly.

An hour later I awoke. I wanted to be sure I beat Jewel out of the bed. I wanted to cook her breakfast before she started her day.

I woke Jewel up to breakfast in bed. Although I'd never said the words, "I'm sorry," this was my way of apologizing. I knew the way to Jewel's heart. With her, it was always the little things that mattered the most. Well, money mattered to her most, but the little things came in a close second.

After breakfast Jewel hopped out of bed and rushed to get to the gym. It was Zumba day, and she didn't want to miss it. Before she left, I gave her a much-needed gift.

"Touch, you're giving me a gun?" Jewel asked with the .22-caliber in her hand.

"Yeah. Bae, I think you really need it. Especially after that baby doll incident. I can't be with you all the time, so you need some extra protection. Besides, that little taser gun you got only works close range."

"All right." Jewel nodded. Then she placed the gun in her purse before heading out the door.

I walked back to the bedroom feeling a little reassured. Now my only worry was that one day Jewel would get the idea to use that same gun on me. I was sure there had been plenty of times she imagined killing me.

Now that I was on my way to patching things up with her, it was on to my next task of the day. I needed to get my car from that crazy bitch, Lisa. I knew the chances of me going to her house and her actually handing the keys over without a fight was slim to none. After her phone call I knew for a fact that she would provoke me to do something terrible to her conniving ass. I definitely didn't need a murder charge on top of domestic abuse and auto theft. The more I thought about it the more it seemed that I was going to have to go over there and meet with her face to face.

Chapter 8

Touch

"Face to Face"

The cab driver out front of my house honked his horn to signal he had arrived and was ready to leave. I opened the door and signaled for him to wait one second. It was the same greasy-haired driver I'd had before, and he didn't look too pleased to have to wait.

As I put my shoes on, I had a decision to make. Do I take my gun to Lisa's house, or do I leave it home? I had been weighing my options ever since I'd called for the cab. On one hand there was no telling what that bitch might come at me with, so it would be good to have protection. On the other hand, I didn't want to get caught with a weapons charge if she saw me coming and called the cops. I wasn't supposed to be anywhere near her, pending the outcome of her case against me.

I grabbed the handle of the gun, paused, then decided it was best to leave it home. The gun found its place next to my underwear in the dresser drawer. I was hoping I had made the right decision by going over to Lisa's unarmed.

On the ride over, I went over every scenario I could think of. I would try and talk sense to her, and hopefully she would give up the car easily. If everything went smooth, then I would be sexing this bitch in a matter of minutes. Give her some good dick then talk her into dropping the charges. If that didn't happen, I didn't have any clue what I would do. I needed to play it right. If the bitch pushed it, I wasn't sure if I could control my temper and not give her a beat-down. Force might be necessary to get my car back.

The cabbie asked, "You want me to come back and pick you up later?"

"Nah. I'm picking my car up. I won't be needing your services ever again." I handed him a twenty-dollar tip.

His eyes bugged out of their sockets. "Too bad. Not everyone tips as good as you. If you ever need a cab, you know who you can call."

I watched him as he drove off down the street. The block was quiet, not a soul around. I looked at Lisa's house and took a deep breath. I tried to keep calm as I walked up to the front door. No use in starting this thing off in a pissed-off mood.

Here we go, I thought as I knocked on the door. I nervously rubbed my hands together as I waited for Lisa to answer. After waiting longer than normal with no answer, I banged on the door a little harder. I looked through the window and didn't see any movement in the house. I went around and looked through the windows of the garage door and saw both Lisa's car and mine. *Why ain't this bitch answering?* I thought.

I circled the house and peeked in all of the windows. Still no sign of Lisa. I had no choice. I was going to have to enter without her permission. What else could I do? She was holding my property, and I needed it back.

Luckily for me I didn't need to break any windows to get in. I knew where Lisa hid her spare key. I was happy not to attract the attention of the neighbors. I reached up and felt around the top of the window frame for the key. *Damn, it's not there!*

I stepped back and looked at the window. I realized I had been feeling around on the wrong one. It was the one closer to the front door. I went to the right window and felt the key immediately.

The key easily slid into the keyhole, and I cautiously and quietly opened the door. Standing just inside the door, I listened carefully but didn't hear anyone moving around the house.

"Yo', Lisa," I yelled.

No answer.

Jackpot! I was going to get my car and all my shit back without having to deal with her crazy ass.

I quickly moved further into the house. My first stop was the kitchen. My car keys were sitting on the counter right where I had left them. I couldn't believe she hadn't even touched them since I had left. In one motion I grabbed the keys and dashed upstairs. I was under a time crunch. I needed to gather all of my belongings and get the hell out before Lisa came home.

The bedroom was a mess, with clothes strewn all over the floor and bed. I opened the door to the equally messy walk-in closet. All of my shoes were under a pile of Lisa's clothes. I threw the clothes into the bedroom and stared at my shoes. I realized I didn't have anything to put my stuff in. The thought of using one of

Lisa's suitcases quickly left my mind. That bitch was likely to say I stole her property and hit me with a burglary and theft charge.

I ran back downstairs and grabbed a few garbage bags from the kitchen. Bounding back up the stairs two at a time, I got a little winded. I paused for a brief moment to catch my breath at the top of the stairs. While standing there, I thought I heard a noise downstairs. I quieted my breathing to pay close attention to the sounds of the house. Satisfied that I was still alone, I continued on, easily filling up two trash bags with my clothes and shoes.

I popped the trunk of my car and threw the bags in and immediately rushed back inside to retrieve the rest of my shit. I still needed to get the flat-screen TV and Blu-ray player I'd bought. Once they were packed in the trunk I slammed it closed. I was just about to get in the car when I remembered the bag of weed I had left behind. *Can't leave the kush behind.* So I went back in one more time.

I came running back down the stairs with the bag of weed in my hand, excited at the thought of getting the hell out of that house and getting high. As soon as I hit the floor at the bottom of the steps, I was attacked from behind.

"What the fuck are you doing in my house?" Lisa jumped on my back like a lioness attacking a gazelle.

I felt my skin break and the blood flow as she sunk her claws into my neck. Caught off guard, the force of her attack knocked me over, and the weed went flying as we both struggled against each other.

Lisa was grabbing, pulling, kicking, clawing whatever she could, to inflict pain. I was trying to regain my bearings and get her off me. She was fighting with the strength of an elephant and the fury of a rabid dog. I was having trouble containing her, and she was getting some solid blows to my head and face. Not only had she scratched my neck, but she drew blood from my ear and ripped my shirt open.

I was finally able to get a good angle on her, and I hauled off on her. The force of my punch sent her flying back.

"You fuckin' crazy?" I screamed.

"What you expect me to do? I go to the store and when I get back there's someone in my house. How you think I'm gonna react?"

"It's me. Not some filthy crackhead breaking into your place."

"You look like a crackhead to me."

"You ain't got to be like that," I said, trying to calm her down.

Her breathing was getting back to a normal rhythm, but she still had a wild look in her eyes.

"Like what? You broke into my house. Fool!" She tried to smooth her wild mane of hair.

"I didn't break in. I used your key to get in. I wanted to surprise you." I took a step toward her.

"You surprised me, all right. I almost killed your ass."

I looked at her seductively and said, "I'd like to kill that ass. Why you think I came over here? I couldn't stand being away from you."

"Oh, yeah?" She smiled.

"I was hoping we could drop all this bullshit between us. Get back to some good lovin' like we used to." I stepped right in on her and stroked her hair.

"We might be able to drop all this. You gonna show me how you want to kill this ass."

I slapped her ass. "You know I do."

"Come on then." She started walking upstairs, and I followed.

When we got to her bedroom, she started walking toward her closet. I needed to stop her before she got inside and saw my shit gone.

"Where you going, bae?" I grabbed her hand.

She pulled away. "I want to put on something sexy for you."

"What for?" I reached for her hand again. "I'll just be taking it off."

"It makes me feel sexy." She avoided my grasp and went to the closet.

It took a second, but then I heard it. "Oh no, you didn't. You muthafucka." She came running out of the closet with a shoe in her hand.

I spun on my heels and darted down the stairs, with Lisa in hot pursuit. I went straight to my car and jumped in.

Lisa came running into the garage with a poker from the fireplace. "You gonna pay, you piece of shit!" she screamed.

I put the car in reverse and was halfway out the garage when Lisa swung and smashed the passenger side window. My tires screeched as I swung out of the driveway and slammed the car into drive, but she was able to smash the rear window as well before I could hit the gas. Her neighbors started coming from their houses.

"You're gonna regret this, Touch! You fucked with the wrong woman! Just you wait!" She threw the poker at my car as I sped down the street.

I looked in my rearview and in the distance saw Lisa still throwing a fit in the middle of the street. This bitch was legit crazy. There was no telling what she was going to come back with. But, at least, I had my car.

Chapter 9

Lisa

"Taking the Law into Your Own Hands"

The color bark brown does my body good in this suit, I thought, admiring myself in my full-length mirror. *It's a shame this is the first time I've ever worn it.* I was dressed professionally with a touch of sexiness. I had to have my boobies hanging out just a little. Give them a little glimpse of what they can't have.

Before I left my apartment, I dabbed Versace Blue Jeans perfume behind my ears and my neck. I got a glimpse of my ass as I walked off. *Hell, if I didn't go super-duper psycho on Touch, he'd still be giving it to me from the back.* That nigga was only good for sex, which was what I craved.

When I walked into the courtroom, the most important eyes I cared about was Touch's. I wanted him to see what he had created and pay for what he had done. No one fucking hits me and gets away with it. He didn't even have the decency to apologize to me. That would have eliminated most of this. On top of that, his dumb ass had made it worse by antagonizing me and breaking into my house. I wanted him to get on his knees to beg for mercy and for my forgiveness. I fell asleep easily at night, knowing Touch wouldn't sleep as he constantly thought about what his new life would be like behind bars.

When I arrived in the courtroom the district attorney with his tuna fish breath pulled me to the side. He wanted to go over some last-minute details. I didn't listen to a word he was saying. I was searching the courtroom for Touch, who was nowhere to be found.

"All rise," the bailiff announced. "The Honorable J.B. Gordon."

I was glad this show was finally starting. I was hoping Touch would be the first to go before the judge, so he could be the first to go to jail. I knew the look on his face would be priceless as soon as the judge announced his guilty verdict. And, after it was all said and done, I had plans to visit him in jail just to laugh and gawk in his face. He had to learn he'd fucked with the wrong one. There was no way he could get away with what he did to me. Touch treated me as if I was a piece of shit. No man had treated me like that, and I wasn't about to allow a man to treat me like that.

I had been sitting on the court bench for over two hours, and my case still hadn't been called. Getting impatient, I looked at my watch. It was eleven-fifteen, and I still hadn't seen Touch. For a minute, I'd begun to think he'd bucked on court and decided to be on the run and leech off another chick, like he'd done me.

I decided to give him another fifteen minutes to show. No such luck. I gathered my things. I wanted to check the docket to be sure I was in the right courtroom.

Just as I was about to stand, the court doors opened, and Touch and his attorney walked through the doors like they owned the place. Touch was decked out in a suit. He walked toward the front of the courtroom with his hot-shot attorney. Our eyes met, and he looked away immediately. He was trying hard not to look my way. I knew he saw me because I was sitting at the end of the bench, near the aisle. I figured he was still pretty pissed off about the baby doll incident and our last altercation at my house.

We weren't called until after the lunch break. Sitting through all that court bullshit wasn't fun at all. And I was anxious to get it over with.

"The Commonwealth calls Lisa Platow to the stand," the bailiff said.

I stood up and walked to the stand like I was walking the runway in Fashion Week. I positioned myself on the witness stand then looked at Touch with piercing eyes. My eyes were glued on him when the bailiff said his spiel about telling the truth, nothing but the truth, blah, blah, blah. Yeah, I agreed and even nodded my head. But I was agreeing to tell my own version of the truth. Like they say, it's three sides to every story, your side, my side and the truth.

"Ms. Platow, would you explain to the court how you received your wounds?" the Commonwealth's Attorney asked.

"The defendant, Trayvon Davis, beat me, punched me, and kicked me, eventually causing me to have a busted nose," I explained through cries. The night before I'd rehearsed this part over and over in the bathroom mirror, hoping the judge would believe me.

"Is this the first time you have been abused by the defendant?"

"No, it isn't." I pulled a handkerchief from my purse and wiped my tears.

"How often would this occur?" The Commonwealth's Attorney was setting it up to go in for the kill.

"He would assault me in some form at least once a week. The simplest things would trigger it. If the defendant had a bad day or I did something that he didn't like, then he would punish me," I lied.

"No further questions, Your Honor."

Next, it was Touch's lawyer's turn to question me. I knew he was about to attempt to dig into my ass, but I was determined not to lose my cool. The last thing I wanted to do was appear as the mad black woman I knew he was gonna try to make me out to be.

"Ms. Platow, how many times have you filed a police report for these so-called occurrences of domestic violence?"

"I'm not sure," I replied, shrugging my shoulders.

"Well, maybe I can help you out. The only police report I see is the one recently filed along with your stolen vehicle. Never once, prior to this incident, did it mention physical violence. Nor did you go to the hospital. There are no hospital reports at all." Touch's lawyer was really making me out to be a liar.

"I told the cop what happened to me. What more do you expect? I was afraid to call the police prior to this incident, and I was too ashamed to go to the hospital." My palms had suddenly become sweaty.

"Ms. Platow, it's clear to me that you're just a scorned woman trying to get back at a man who you're in love but who's not in love with you."

This lawyer was getting under my skin. Because I was afraid what may come out of my mouth, I remained silent, but I was sure my thoughts were written all over my face as I rolled my eyes.

"Your Honor, based on the huge lack of physical evidence, I move to dismiss this case. This case is frivolous and an obvious fraud." Touch's lawyer walked away.

"Ms. Platow, you may step down," the judge ordered.

As I started to walk back to my seat, I realized I had just lost this battle. My hands couldn't stop shaking, not to mention my sweaty palms. Before taking my seat, I cut my eyes at Touch one last time, who sat calmly with a smirk across his face. The mere sight of his smug little ass made my blood boil.

"Please rise for the verdict," the judge announced.

I listened as the judge announced a not guilty verdict for the assault charge and guilty for the stolen vehicle charge. He was sentenced to one year supervised probation. I couldn't believe my ears. Even if Touch was found not guilty on the assault charge, I at least expected him to get time for stealing my damn car.

I grabbed my purse and began to storm out of the courtroom. I met Touch at the courtroom door. "After you," he said then began to laugh.

"Fuck you, Touch!" I yelled, totally losing my mind.

That laugh in my face was the last straw. I took off my five-inch stiletto heels and started beating Touch with it. I got in a few good jabs in his dick and face. Before I knew it, he had begun to bleed, and the bailiff was all over me. Before he was able to pry me off him, I'd managed to bite Touch in the face. The bailiff had saved him this time, but it wasn't over. This was just the beginning. I had it in for Touch, and he was gonna pay. I'd decided to take justice into my own hands. After I made bail and got myself out for contempt of court. Now I was doubly pissed.

Chapter 10

Jewel

"Woman of Destruction"

My hands were starting to cramp as I sorted Touch's money into stacks of ones, fives, tens, twenties, and hundreds. It seemed like the stack of ones was always the smallest. Although I knew it wasn't right, and to some it may even be stealing, I would always take most of Touch's one-dollar bills for myself. By the time I was done, I'd have at least two hundred dollars in ones alone. Believe it or not, he never even missed them. As far as I was concerned, Touch owed me, and I deserved a little gift. Over time those extra ones added up to designer handbags, jeans, and shoes that I loved. And I never once took a fifty or a hundred-dollar bill. I knew my limit, and I wasn't about to push it.

After I separated the money and marked the large bills with a counterfeit pen, I slid it through the money counter. I thought back to those times I used to count each bill by hand. Talk about carpel tunnel and some major hand cramps! It took quite a bit of begging, but Touch finally bought a money counter.

Once I verified the amount and strapped it, I placed the money aside. Then I pulled out all the bills for the month and totaled them up. Things had really gotten behind, with Touch being on the run and then locked up. I was slowly getting out of debt with all the money coming in and was grateful that our bills were finally getting caught up. We would have been out of debt much sooner, but you know I needed to pamper myself. A girl needs her bags, shoes, jewelry, and clothes.

With Touch being in the drug name, it wasn't wise to put anything in his name, so everything fell on me. As soon as we stopped paying the bills, collectors were after me like I'd stolen something. My credit was ruined, and my bank account had a lien.

So I nearly jumped for joy as I grabbed enough money to pay all our past due bills in full. I counted out bills money and put the rest of the money in the vault in the basement. I walked to the vault with a permanent smile on my face.

I know people say money can't buy happiness, but it sure does make things a lot easier in life. Which in turn gives happiness. Not only that, money is the number one reason marriages fall apart, so what does that tell you? I noticed since Touch had been making a little money, things between us were getting a little better. Our relationship wasn't the best, and we definitely still had our issues, but things were a little brighter. At least we had hope at this point. I still didn't feel we had gained back that love we'd had in the past, and we still weren't quite that dynamic duo of a team as we were in the past either. But I was grateful and hopeful that we were slowly making progress.

Rico had stopped calling and harassing me. Plus, those crazy-ass anonymous calls had ceased as well. I was no longer afraid to go outside to get the mail anymore or packing my gun just to go to the grocery store. I was even starting to feel safe without Touch in the house. I was feeling so good that I'd decided to do something special for him.

I whipped up a T-bone steak and scrambled eggs with cheese, his all-time favorite meal. I purposely had a grill built into the kitchen stovetop. It was nights like these that it came in handy. I popped open a bottle of Moët to enjoy with our meal and lit candles in the dining room, kitchen, bedroom, and even the stairs. Then I turned on some jazz music to create a relaxed mood in the house.

I didn't want to say much to Touch, except how much I truly loved him. Enjoying our food and riding the shit out of him was what both of us needed.

I threw on a flaming red lingerie set I'd ordered from Victoria's Secret and matching five-inch stilettoes. It was something about the color red that sent Touch into a sexual rage.

Just as I was finishing up the meal preparation I heard Touch pull up in the driveway. I turned down the lights and lit the candles on the table. The ones I placed throughout the house were already full flame. I was in need of Touch's dick. I was feeling an attraction for him I hadn't felt in a long time. Maybe it had something to do with all of the sexiness I had created in the house. It even made me think that just maybe the love was coming back.

I hurried to the bathroom to freshen up and give myself a quick look-over. When I was done Touch still hadn't come in the house. I began to get anxious, so I looked out of the window to see what was taking him so damn long. Touch had just gotten out the car, and to my surprise he had roses in his hands. I smiled, knowing this was going to be a good night for us.

I watched as Touch headed toward the front door. After he took only a few steps, I watched him fall down on the ground like he had been shot. Without thinking I grabbed the gun he gave me from the kitchen drawer. I rushed outside with gun cocked, ready to blast the first thing moving. As soon as I took a few steps out the door, out jumped a chick from the bushes with a huge gun the size of a rifle in her hand laughing hysterically. I didn't know what the hell was so funny, and I didn't have time to try and figure it out. I aimed at her without hesitation and pulled the trigger.

Pow!

I opened my eyes after shooting the gun. To my surprise the chick was still standing there. Evidently my aim wasn't as good as I thought. Guess next time I should keep my eyes open when I fire.

"You crazy bitch!" The girl dropped her gun and hit the ground, covering up in a ball.

I was struggling to cock my gun again and put another bullet in the chamber when I heard Touch scream out, "Jewel, don't! It's not a real gun! She only has a BB gun!" He snatched the gun from me.

That's when I realized what was going on. This bitch had to be none other than Lisa. I picked up a tree branch and started running in her direction. Realizing she was about to get a beat-down of a lifetime, she ran toward her car.

"Your charges may have went away, but don't think I'm going to do the same!" Lisa screamed at the top of her lungs as she got in her car and sped off.

I chased after her. It didn't take me long to recognize I wouldn't catch her, so I gave up. I was furious as I stood in the middle of the street yelling all sorts of profanities at the top of my lungs. I was half-naked and making a fool out of myself in front of my neighbors. I began to walk back to the house, preparing to dig into Touch's ass.

"Jewel!" Touch yelled as I walked back toward the house. "Jewel!" he screamed again and began to rush toward me. "Jewel!" He tackled me to the ground like a football player.

"What the—"

Zoom! A car sped by, interrupting my sentence.

Touch had just saved my life, pushing me out of the path of Lisa's vehicle. That psycho bitch was trying to run me over. That was it. She had finally pushed me to the limit. I wanted to grab my gun and shoot that bitch between her eyes just for fucking with us. I couldn't believe she had the nerve to come to my house. Then I began to wonder how she knew where I lived. My brain became flooded with all sorts of thoughts as I had a flashback to that baby doll incident.

"I can't take this shit no more!" I shoved Touch off of me with all my force. "Because of you thinking with your dick, you put my life in danger. Dumb ass! What if that car had actually hit me? And what if Lisa had a real gun?" I stood to my feet and began to walk away.

"Make her ass go away, Touch," I yelled, looking back at Touch, who was a couple feet behind me.

"It's not that easy, Jewel," Touch mumbled back.

"What do you mean? I've seen you make much bigger problems disappear. Why is Lisa any different? What? You got feelings for her or something?" I demanded to know as we walked in the house.

"Jewel, you're talking crazy. Don't worry. I got this. Go upstairs and lay down. You don't need to be getting all upset. It's not good for the baby."

"Good for the baby? Are you fuckin' serious?" I got up in Touch's face. "How the fuck you gon' part your lips and tell me what's good for a damn baby? Me nearly getting ran over by a fuckin' car isn't good for the fuckin' baby. Nigga, please! Get the fuck outta here!" I shoved Touch in the head.

"Don't put your hands on me, Jewel," Touch said, grabbing my wrist. He had a death grip on it, and I could feel my fingers getting numb from lack of blood flow.

"Or what?" I knew he was serious, but there was no way I was backing down. I was just as mad as he was and ready for war.

"Fuck this!" Touch said then pushed me into the wall while attempting to walk away.

As an immediate reaction, I started punching him in the chest. I had so much pent up aggression, and I was letting it all out on him.

"Jewel, stop!" Touch demanded as he tried holding me down.

"Why don't you stop acting like a fuckin' little bitch and start being a man? The old Touch would have never allowed this to happen. On top of that, I know this ain't the first time that bitch has been here. This is just the first time I've caught you and the bitch in action. Fuck you! You could never be the father of my damn child!"

Those were the last words I spoke before Touch scooped me up and slammed me on the table. I hit my head so hard that I was dizzy. Before that I'd always thought that seeing stars was a figure of speech, but now I know it's real.

I grabbed my head as I rose to my feet and noticed my hand was soaked in blood. Once I realized I was bleeding, it was like I'd immediately become possessed by a demon. I ran to the kitchen and grabbed the first thing I saw. Lucky for Touch it was only a meat pulverizer, but I'd planned to pulverize his ass to death.

"Jewel, put that down, please. I'm sorry," he began to beg. "Ah, damn! Baby, you're bleeding bad. Let me help you." Touch tried coming near me with a towel in hand.

"Don't come near me!"

"Jewel, I know you're mad, and so am I. But right now you're bleeding really bad. Please, baby, let me help you." Touch attempted to grab my arm.

"Get the fuck away from me!" I yelled like a crazed woman then started hitting him all over with the meat tenderizer. The blows landed with thuds. If his arms were a steak, they would be the most tender cut of meat you ever tasted.

When my arms got too tired to swing anymore, I dropped my weapon and ran upstairs. I didn't know where I was going, but my first instinct was to pack my bags, so that's what I did. Touch gave a half-hearted attempt to try and stop me, and that pissed me off even more. Instead he just stood there and watched me pack. I was in a daze as I packed and didn't even realize what I was packing, but once all of my Louis Vuitton bags were full, I grabbed them and headed out the door.

"Jewel," Touch called out to me in his most pitiful tone.

He even sounded like he was crying, but I refused to look in his direction. Keeping my eyes focused on the door only, I walked right past him and into the garage. I hopped in my car and pulled out the driveway, never looking back.

"Where the hell am I going to go now?" I shouted at the top of my lungs, tears streaming down my face. For thirty minutes I'd been driving in circles with no place to go. It was times like this I wish I had my mom to run to. My mom had moved back home to Panama years earlier, and not a day went by that I didn't think of her and miss her. She'd taught me all I needed to know about being the materialistic, gold-digging woman I was. I knew she was only a phone call away, but I didn't want to call her with this mess because she would be worried. There was nothing she could've done to help me at that point, and hearing her voice would have only made me sad.

I became lost in my thoughts as I hopped on the interstate, feeling alone and sorry for myself. Everyone I let close to me always let me down.

Sasha, that conniving bitch that pretended to be in love with me, was the first to fuck me over. Then came Misty, who was the perfect friend and played the role so well, I totally forgot Sasha existed. Well, little

miss perfect turned out to be a cop. My first true love,
Calico, was simply using me to move drugs for him.
Finally, there's Touch, my best friend turned lover,
who fucked me over more times than I can count.

The more I thought, the more realized the poor choices I'd made in friends and men. I couldn't understand how one person could get dealt such a bad hand in life. Why was I always letting people take advantage of me? Why did I put myself in these positions? Well, I'd had enough. I was no longer going to be taken advantage of. I turned up my radio and drove along with a renewed confidence.

Before long I'd gotten so wrapped up in the tunes of my iPod that I hadn't even realized 64 West had turned into 95 South, and it was getting close to midnight. Here I was in the middle of nowhere in the middle of the night. I was exhausted and needed a place to crash. Since Touch had been watching me pack, I wasn't able to take all of my cash during my rush to get out of the house. I didn't want to spend a chunk of the money I did have on some fleabag motel.

I wracked my brain trying to think of someone I knew in the area. That's when it hit me—my girl Shakira. She had recently moved to DC. Although I hadn't talked to her in nearly two years, she was my last option. Shakira and I were really close, but our friendship became distant due to the jealous ways of a previous friend of mine, Sasha. Sasha had played me and actually made me think I might be in love with her for a minute. Her conniving, jealous ass got in between Shakira and me and caused us to lose touch with one another. I'd always regretted not patching things up with

Shakira, but I was too embarrassed to admit that Shakira had been right about Sasha's sneaky ass. Shakira had warned me, but I didn't listen. I was too stubborn.

Then when everything started happening with Touch and Calico, I got so caught up that patching things up with Shakira was the last thing on my mind. Sometimes I felt so dumb when I thought about the decisions I made. Actually I attributed a lot of my heartache to Sasha. There weren't many things I could say I regretted, but being friends with her was definitely a big, big mistake.

I grabbed my phone to give Shakira a call, but I noticed I had ten missed calls and six text messages from Touch. My radio was turned up so loud and I was so lost in thought, I hadn't heard any of his attempts. Deep inside I wanted to call him back, but I just couldn't allow myself to do it. I truly felt he was probably still fucking with Lisa. Too bad for him he found out the hard way she had a touch of fatal attraction.

I scrolled to Shakira's number in my cell phone. For a moment I contemplated whether I should make the call or not. I felt guilty for letting time get away from our friendship, but I trusted she was the kind of friend who, if we hadn't talked in a while, would just pick up where we left off. With that final thought, I pressed send.

"Hello," she answered.

"Hi, Shakira. It's me, Jewel," I said softly, unsure how she would respond.

"It's who?" she asked in a groggy tone.

"Jewel."

"Oh, Jewel! Girl, I didn't recognize your voice. Is everything okay?" she asked right away. It was amazing how she still could sense something was wrong, even though we hadn't talked in ages.

"Honestly, I'm not okay." I began to cry all over again.

"Aaaawwww, Jewel. What's wrong, honey?"

"It's a long story. My life is in shambles. I just packed up and left Virginia Beach. I've been riding for hours. I'm in your area. Do you mind if I come over just for the night?" I said, just putting it out there. I was so exhausted, I didn't bother beating around the bush.

"Sure. When we hang up, I will text you my address, and you can just put it in your navigation system. I'll be waiting for you. Drive carefully."

"Thank you so much," I responded, grateful she was my savior in a time of need.

My attention was directed toward my dashboard after hanging up the phone with Shakira. I had fifty miles before empty. I was feeling tired and drained, so I figured this was probably the best time to pull off, get gas, a 5-hour Energy, and wait for Shakira's text.

I stopped at the BP gas station directly off the exit. My stomach had started feeling queasy, so I used the bathroom and grabbed a snack.

Emotionally, physically, and mentally drained from the day, I was totally exhausted and in a daze as I set the pump and got back in the car.

"Get the hell out of the car!" a man demanded, gun in hand.

"What!" I replied.

My head was spinning. I must have dozed off while waiting for the gas to finish pumping.

"Now!" he demanded.

I gathered myself and jumped out the car as the masked man demanded. I contemplated running away but was afraid he would shoot me if I tried.

He immediately started rummaging through my car. He used one hand to snatch my iPod while using the other to keep the gun pointed directly at me.

My hands began trembling, and my bladder was about to burst. I closed my eyes and silently prayed this dude would take whatever he wanted and leave me alone. I didn't want my life to end this way.

I heard another male voice directly behind me say, "Yo', come on, man. People are coming."

I was relieved that I hadn't tried to run. I probably would have been gunned down by whoever was behind me.

"Shit!" The masked man rushed out my car. He pressed the gun firmly against my temple and down to my neck. "Turn your face," he said. "Don't look at me!"

I closed my eyes and did exactly what he said. The next thing I could hear was him getting into another vehicle and driving away. I let out a sigh of relief as I opened my eyes to see nothing but his mask lying on the ground. My life had been spared, and he hadn't gotten away with anything but an iPod. I was certain God had left me here for a reason.

Just then I felt my phone vibrate in my pocket. Shakira's text had come through. I plugged the address into the navigation system and headed down the road to my new life.

Chapter 11

Unknown Person

"On a Mission"

My counselor asked me, "Are you ready to say the sobriety prayer?"

"Yes." I nodded.

This would be the last time I would say that damn prayer and the last time I would see that group. Sad to say, as much I hated that place, I sure was going to miss them, especially my counselor, Frank. He had really helped me get through some hard times. My final night in the center they threw a small party for me. The best part was the confetti cake from Cold Stone Ice Cream Bakery. Even though to this day I felt like I never should have been there, I must say, while there, I learned to enjoy the simple pleasures of life.

Before arriving at the center, the police force was my life. Working undercover and taking down the bad guys was what kept me going each day. But when I pissed off one of my superiors and they tried to force me onto desk duty, I fought back. So when I got into an accident, they really fucked with me and told the public I had been killed.

Then when they saw I wasn't going away, they went on to say I had drugs and alcohol in my system and hid me in a rehab center. Of course I had drugs and alcohol in my system, I was undercover. I had to do what the people around me were doing. That wasn't uncommon in my line of work at all. What it all boiled down to was, they wanted me off the force, and they were going to get me off by all means. I knew the justice system was crooked, but I never expected to be a victim. After all, I was on their side.

As I walked out of the treatment center, I could only imagine my family or anyone at all coming to greet me outside. With my career as my primary focus, I had no time for children, a mate, or even a pet companion. No one would be coming to greet my sorry ass. The one relationship I did have ended when my life on the force began. Every other relationship I had was all related to my work, so none of it seemed real. During my time at the treatment center I realized there was one person who I might have had some real feelings for.

My reality hit me as I got outside of the building. Nothing but the dust from the cab stopping and greeting me. I said hello and hopped in. As I got comfortable, I was hit with a stench of sweat and smoke in the car. That's when I realized I was entering back into the real world after a year and a half in rehab. The ride home was surreal. I felt like the world had already changed so much. In fact, it wasn't the world that had changed, it was me. I was clean and sober.

When I arrived home, I was in total shock. As I walked into my apartment, chills went down my spine. It had been so long since I'd been there, for a moment

I felt like I was in an unfamiliar place. That feeling quickly went away as soon as I entered the living room. I stared at the countless plaques and honors on my wall. They reminded me of what I used to be. As I went down the row of plaques, it was a virtual walk down memory lane. I thought back to the many cases I had solved and the awards ceremonies.

There were definitely more highs than lows throughout my career, but the most recent and lasting memory was the lowest of the low. I was forced off my case and out of the department.

Thinking of all that went wrong made me feel like a failure. A rush of anger came over me, and I grabbed the largest garbage bag I could find and began to throw all the plaques and awards in there. None of them meant shit at that point.

I'd worked so hard and was so committed to the force, just to have everything blow up in my face in the end really hurt. At first, I wanted to die, but deep inside I knew I couldn't give up so easily. I needed to survive this ordeal, so I could redeem myself. So I could repair my reputation.

The first thing I learned in rehab was that love truly conquers all. From that day I knew I had to go to my special person to confess my everlasting love. The thought of this person was what helped me make it through. Since I no longer had the force to look forward to, I made this person my daily motivation. There was one problem—I had met this person on the job, and we had left on very bad terms.

After clearing my wall of every honor and plaque I'd received, I went into the bathroom. All I wanted to do was take a hot shower and wash away the past. The grime and dirt of my past were weighing me down, and I needed it lifted. I stopped and looked at myself in the mirror. I hated the person I saw. I saw a failure.

Looking in the medicine cabinet, I found a pair of sharp scissors and started cutting my hair then I dyed it platinum blonde. This was going to be a new beginning. I never again wanted to be reminded of who I used to be. Finally after cleaning up all the stray hairs that had fallen in the sink, I took a shower in the hottest temperature I could stand. I stood there watching the past fall away right down the drain. It was a new day.

After my shower I headed into my kitchen and opened the refrigerator. The stench of moldy milk, cheese, strawberries, and Chinese food almost made me vomit. Again I found myself grabbing a garbage bag. Just like my awards, I tossed everything from the fridge in there.

It didn't take long for me to realize my whole place needed a thorough cleaning, so I turned on the radio and got to it. I cleaned my apartment from top to bottom. When I was done, the place smelled of bleach. I grabbed my bags of garbage and headed to the dumpster. On the way there, I was stopped in the hallway by a voice calling to me from behind. My old self would have been on high alert if someone had called me from behind, but the new me was calm.

"Excuse me," a familiar voice said.

I turned around to see the previous love of my life. I was no longer calm. My heart began to beat hard, and a lump formed in my throat.

"Hey," I was so caught off guard, it was the only word I managed to get out.

"Oh, that's the best greeting you can give an old friend?" Jamie said to me while we embraced.

I could have stayed in Jamie's arms forever. It had been so long since I'd felt the loving embrace of a mate. I had no idea what to say to him. We stood there for a second until Jamie broke the tension by grabbing one of the garbage bags I was carrying.

Jamie and I had been lovers for three years. It was a typical passionate affair that just lost its passion. Well, *I* lost my passion for it. I fell in love with something new, my job. I just didn't have time for Jamie anymore. My new lover was more exciting and dangerous. Seeing Jamie brought up so many memories, good and bad. All the bad memories had to do with the way I'd treated him toward the end of the relationship. I didn't know any other way to handle the situation than to be a bitch and make him hate me. I was hoping that Jamie wasn't here to bring up old fights and make me beg for forgiveness.

"So what brings you here, old friend?" I asked Jamie as we headed to the dumpster together.

"You. I've been keeping up with you. I heard you had been in rehab for a while and you were getting out today, so I wanted to be there to welcome you home. I actually went up to the facility to pick you up, but you had already gone."

"Oh, that was nice of you. I would have never expected to see you." I smiled at Jamie. The thought that he still cared enough to want to meet me made me happy inside. I guess he had forgiven me for my attitude all those years ago.

"So how are you? It's been so long. Did rehab help?"

"I think so. I've turned over a new leaf in my life. I'm feeling clear and conscious for the first time in a long time."

"That's great. Rehab did all that?"

"Yep. I learned to slow down and take it one day at a time. If I don't get it done instantly, I won't die."

"I agree. I haven't learned to accept that concept yet. Maybe you could help me with it."

Jamie never was the type to wait to see how things would work out when faced with a problem. With the smallest obstacle, he would run like a puppy with its tail between its legs. That's one reason why we never worked out. I loved a challenge and faced them head on, even if sometimes too fast and without thinking it all the way through. It was the only way I knew how to operate. Frankly I thought it was kind of bitch-like to run from your problems.

"Listen, umm, I'm starving. Did you have dinner yet?" Jamie asked with a rub to the tummy.

"What are you in the mood for?"

"Pizza loaded with cheese and sausage," Jamie said right away.

"I see nothing has changed." I smiled. "Still the same Jamie."

"You remembered?" Jamie smiled back.

"How could I forget? Now come on up to my place. Lucky for you, I just finished cleaning my house, so I won't need to put your ass to work." I laughed.

Jamie said, "I'm guessing your apartment reeks of bleach."

"Yes, it does." I giggled. "Guess I'm not the only one that remembers old habits."

"Some things in our relationship I will never forget," Jamie said.

We ordered a pizza covered in hot Italian sausage and roasted red peppers. Seeing Jamie again was quite comforting. It was easy to fall right back into a rhythm with him. It was familiar and safe, which was what I really craved at that moment.

After coming out of the rehab center, I thought no one would grace me with their presence. For my whole stay in rehab I thought I was alone, but I had come to accept that. Then out of nowhere came Jamie. I knew one thing for sure, things happen for a reason. I sat there thinking that maybe Jamie and I were supposed to rekindle our relationship, get married, and have a puppy.

We sat there for a good hour just talking and laughing. It was a nice way to reenter society.

"So, what bring you back here, Jamie?" I asked before picking up our plates and placing them in the sink. After Jamie and I had broken up he had moved out of town. He said he had another job in Baltimore, but I figured he was leaving to get away from me. Thinking about it made me feel a bit guilty, but I can't control how other people react.

"I landed a corporate position with a cigarette company in sales and marketing. I couldn't refuse the offer that was on the table. I just moved back. Haven't even been here two days. I'm not even unpacked yet. Boxes are all over my apartment."

"Knowing how you are, they will be there for a while." I laughed.

It felt so good to laugh and be at ease, it was easy for me to fall into Jamie arms. It felt so comforting. It turned me on to be wrapped up in another person's arms again.

Even though, I wasn't ready for sex, we did mess around. Jamie couldn't get enough of my clit. Having an orgasm relieved a lot of tension for me. It had been a while since anyone had been down there, besides my own fingers. After we both had our orgasms, I invited Jamie to stay over for the night.

The next morning I woke up to see Jamie's head on the pillow next to mine. It wasn't until that moment I realized that I'd possibly made a big mistake. I hadn't even been home twenty-four hours and I already had a regret.

This was not the love I'd planned to come home to. It wasn't the thought of reuniting with Jamie that kept me going while in rehab. I wanted to reunite with Jewel. The thought of her was what kept me going.

My stomach started to turn as I thought about how I'd just fucked up. I had to get Jamie out of my house and fast. I needed more time alone to think about what I was doing with my life. What was going to make me happiest? I thought Jewel was going to make me happiest, but now this little encounter had me all messed up.

"Good morning, baby," I whispered, to wake Jamie.

"Good morning," Jamie said between yawns.

"Not to rush you out the door, but I've got an appointment I have to rush to this morning," I lied.

"Oh, no problem," Jamie said while getting up.

As Jamie got dressed, I went to the bathroom to brush my teeth and wash my face. I had to make it look authentic. I waited in the bathroom for a few minutes extra to give Jamie some time to get dressed and me some time to get my head straight. By the time I returned to the bedroom Jamie was fully dressed.

"Can I leave you my number?" Jamie asked with cell phone in hand.

"Sure." I grabbed my phone and entered the numbers as Jamie called them out to me.

"Will you call me later?" Jamie asked before heading toward the door.

I nodded. "Yes."

"I'm going to be totally honest with you—I want this relationship back," Jamie said, looking me in the eyes and cradling my face.

That was the last thing I expected or wanted him to say. "Let me think about it. I don't want us to move too fast," was the best response I could come up with.

I did enjoy Jamie's company, but I wasn't sure I was ready to rekindle what we had in the past. Too much had transpired, and so much time had passed. We were both different people from back then. I was dealing with personal issues, which I wasn't sure I could do if I had to worry about someone else's issues as well. I looked at life through a different window than when Jamie and I were dating.

"Understandable," Jamie said.

After exchanging a small kiss, we gave each other a big hug, and I watched as Jamie walked through the front door of my apartment. I sat on my couch and tried to figure out why my life seemed to be so complicated. Less than a day from rehab and already I was dealing with drama. I sighed as my thoughts went to Jewel.

Chapter 12

Touch

"You've Got Balls"

"Here you go, Officer Phelps," I said, handing him a fresh box of Krispy Kreme doughnuts. The box also included ten crisp hundred-dollar bills. I laughed to myself as I wondered what it was with piggies and their beloved doughnuts.

Jimmy had at least ten cops on his payroll. When they saw us doing our thing in the streets, they kindly looked the other way. These dudes were even willing to get rid of a body for Jimmy. This kid, Officer Phelps, was a street kid turned cop. He said Jimmy was like a father to him. The longer I worked for Jimmy, the more I realized that this man was and will always be loved in the streets.

Officer Phelps took the box without a word. He opened it up, took out a doughnut, and started eating it. I believe he was just making sure the money was in there. He kept eating the doughnut as he walked away.

I got in my truck and headed back to the spot.

"It's a wrap for tonight," Deuce said, nodding his head as we gathered up Jimmy's cut.

I wrapped the money tight and handed it over to him, so he could make the drop to Jimmy's girl. Happy to be done for the day, I got ghost quick. No way I was going to hang around and have Deuce think of one last errand for me to run.

That night when I got home, I puffed on a couple of blunts while listening to some music. Listening to those songs really had me reminiscing. It seemed every song that came up reminded me of Jewel. Damn, I was missing that girl. Since I hadn't heard from her, I figured she had finally reached her breaking point.

Usually she would have either come home by now or at least contacted me, considering I had blown up her phone with texts and voice mails. I knew I'd done it this time, so I can't say that I blame her. How much can one person take? Truth is, I knew I could be a motherfucking handful at times.

I got so high, I passed out on the couch before I could call Jewel and tell her once more how much I missed her.

The next morning, I got up and went to Waffle House to eat pancakes, and scrambled eggs with cheese and bacon. I was really starting to miss Jewel bad. This used to be one of our favorite breakfast spots. To cheer my spirits up, I went to visit Jimmy. He was turning into a father figure for me. I wish our visits didn't have to be in a prison separated by plexiglass. To maintain a low profile, we would make our conversations brief. Talking in codes made both of us feel a little at ease. No matter how low you talk, you never know who may be listening. Especially the bullshit warden.

"What's up, Jimbo!" I said as soon as Jimmy walked to the glass window.

"You know what it is, youngblood," Jimmy said as he sat down.

"You looking good."

"Yeah, I'd be looking better on the other side of this glass though." Jimmy grinned. "So how's business?"

"Business is good. We're getting the goods in regularly, and the customers are happy. No complaints, boss." I tried my best to answer Jimmy without saying too much.

"And what about the employees, are they staying in line? They coming to work on time and paying off their debts?"

I assured Jimmy everything was in line. "Everything's in order, boss. Don't you worry."

"That's what I like to hear."

Jimmy and I talked about the latest on the streets, and the latest jail talk, then wrapped up our visit. It was always good talking with Jimmy. He gave me good advice and made sure I understood everything that was going on. He had a knack for making me feel better. He was a smart old dude, and I loved learning from him. He was quick with dropping his knowledge on me, and I soaked it all up. He had lived through it all and seen it all, so the dude knew what he was talking about.

After visiting Jimmy, I went back to the crib. I didn't have any work for the day, so I was gonna just relax. Getting some rest was long overdue for me. I had been grinding nonstop for a while and was exhausted.

I was looking forward to a little rest and relaxation, but to my surprise, I couldn't relax at all. My mind was churning with thoughts about Jewel. It had come to the point that everything in the house reminded me of her. Everywhere I looked, there was another memory of her.

I couldn't take it anymore. I dialed Jewel's cell number. The tough guy role was out the door. No more pride for this lion. I repeatedly kept calling her, leaving voice mails and sending loving texts. But no matter how many phone calls or texts I sent, I still got no response. After a while I was actually starting to worry. This was not like Jewel.

I looked at the clock, and it was only seven in the evening. I couldn't sit in the crib any longer. I had been pacing around the house all day and needed some different scenery. My weed was done, and I didn't have shit to drink. Thinking about Jewel and being dry was gonna drive a nigga crazy.

With that, I grabbed my jacket and keys and headed out the door. I was gonna hit a local bar for a few drinks. Hopefully being around people would get my mind off Jewel. Jewel had some crazy-ass hold on a nigga, and I needed to break her grip.

As soon as I walked out the door, I saw a midnight blue Jag pull up in my driveway. I didn't recognize the car and wasn't expecting anyone. I was immediately on guard. My thoughts raced as to who it could be. Was it Lisa? Was it one of Jimmy's associates? Whoever it was, I wasn't getting a good feeling and wasn't in the mood for no bullshit.

"Get the fuck off my property," I stated, pulling my gun from my waist.

"Yo', man. I didn't come here to start any shit," a male voice said. "I just want to know if Jewel is here."

"Who the fuck are you?" I asked with a mean-mug face.

"Rico," he replied.

So this is the muthafucka Jewel had been spending all her time with when I was locked up, I thought. As soon as I heard the name I already knew who he was. I finally was able to put a face to the name. *This muthafucka has some nerve coming to my crib.*

"You got two options, dude. You can get in your car and leave my property, or leave this earth. Which one will it be?" I asked, putting the gun to his temple.

"It's cool, my nig. I'll leave." Rico got back in his car and put the window down. "Just do me a favor and tell Jewel I came by. By the way, you need to be a little more kind to your savior. If it wasn't for me, your ass would still be in that cell, homie. You never know when you may need me again." Then he sped off.

Once I was sure Rico was gone, I texted Jewel, telling her what had just gone down. Of course when she received that text, she called back right away. It pissed me off how she didn't respond when I was spilling my heart out to her, but she wasted no time calling back about Rico. She called me back to back three times in a row before I finally decided to answer.

"Tell me right now what went down with you and Rico," I demanded as soon as I answered the phone. "This nigga coming to my house looking for you and shit."

"Lower your voice, Touch, or I'm hanging up!" Jewel yelled back.

I ignored her ass because I knew if we were face to face, she definitely would not be acting this gangsta. In fact if she did step to me this way in person, I would have likely slapped her upside her head. No one was allowed to step to me with that attitude and not get checked back into place.

I began to say, "I'm only going to ask you one more time—"

Jewel interrupted me. "He was there for me when you were not, and it was his money that got your sorry ass out of jail. That's all you need to know." She then hung up the phone.

I called her ass back at least ten times, but I got no response. After the second attempt at calling her, she turned her phone off, but I still continued to blow up her voice mail. After a while I gave up.

I sped to the bar angry that I had spilled my heart to Jewel and all she could do was hang up in my face. I needed a drink and fast. Once I reached the bar I threw back shot after shot until I could no longer feel the burn. My anger, pain and hurt had been numbed. I sat there and let the liquor work its magic on my nerves and emotions. When I was completely numb and totally fucked up, I looked at the bartender, tried to order another round, and passed out. That's the last thing I remembered about that night.

The next morning, I woke up not knowing how the hell I got home. I assumed the bartender either called a cab or took me home himself. I was going to have to get my truck later on. I was thankful for a new day and ready to get on my grind and make some money.

A half-finished blunt was sitting on my nightstand. I lit it up and took a few pulls as I gathered my morning thoughts. As I sat on my bed puffing on the blunt, I heard the toilet flush. I jumped out the bed and raced to the bathroom. I opened the door, and there was a woman standing at the sink.

"Hey." She smiled.

"I'm sorry, but who the fuck are you? And how did you get into my house?"

"Ah, I'm the one who got your ass home from the bar."

Damn, I was fucked up last night! I don't remember talking to this bitch at all. "Okay, that's cool, but I don't know you and you need to get your ass out my house."

"Nigga, please. You don't have to ask me twice. Your ass was so lame last night, I can't wait to never see your ass again."

"Fuck you, bitch! You pushin' it."

She sauntered past me like she didn't have a care in the world and walked downstairs. I followed and watched as she put her shoes on and made her way to the front door. She turned before she went out and said, "You're welcome for getting you home safe. Your truck is in the garage. I took what you owe me and nothing more."

"What the fuck you talking about?"

"I'm a prostitute, you fool. I don't give this pussy up for free. Well, last night I didn't give it up. I have two words for you—*whisky dick.*" She smiled and closed the door in my face.

She was so calm about the whole thing, it left me tongue-tied. I had nothing to say to her. She had stunned me and left me standing at the door trying to make sense of what she just told me. It took me a little bit, but I realized I had just been suckered and dissed by a prostitute.

Instead of getting mad at the prostitute, I directed my anger at Jewel. She still hadn't come home. I knew her crazy ass was heated, but so was I. My baby had never stayed away from home so long, but I sure as hell wasn't going to give her what she wanted. I figured she probably had the phone right by her side waiting for me to call and make up.

I almost called her but then thought better of it. *Naw, man, I believe I'm going to wait this one out.* I just knew deep inside my baby would be walking through the house door any day now telling me how much she missed me and loved me. Or at least I was hoping she would.

In an attempt to kill time and get Jewel off my mind, I popped in a DVD featuring comedian Mike Epps. He was so funny that my stomach cramped up as I watched him act a damn fool in the movie *Friday*. It didn't' take long for the munchies to kick in, so I made my famous turkey sandwich to tide me over.

By the time I finished eating, it was going on one o'clock in the afternoon, and I still hadn't heard from Jewel. Unable to resist any longer, my fingers began to dial her cell number. Again, it went straight to voice mail. "What the hell!" I shouted out to no one in particular.

I dialed Jewel's number three more times to make sure my hearing was correct. Each time I got the same message, "You have reached the automated voice mail box of—"

"This chick cut her phone off," I said as I pressed end on my cell phone.

The more I sat and let shit marinate, the angrier I got. I couldn't stand it. I called Jewel again.

"Yo', Jewel, stop playing. This ain't funny. Bring your ass home. You taking this shit way too far," I screamed in the phone, leaving her a voice mail, then threw my cell phone across the room.

All this stress about Jewel was fucking me up. My temples were pounding, and it felt like my head was gonna explode in a matter of seconds. A headache was coming toward my temples and fast. I decided to lay down and take a nap before I lost my mind and totally flipped out.

When I woke back up, I turned over to look at the time on the clock. It was getting close to eight o'clock. My whole day was wasted worrying about this bitch. I went across the room and grabbed my cell phone from the floor where it had landed when I threw it earlier. I checked the caller ID, and there still was no call from Jewel, but I refused to give her the satisfaction of me calling again. Jewel loved to see me squirm.

She had never been this stubborn, so I was beginning to get a little worried. I was hoping nothing had happened to her. Quickly erasing those thoughts from my mind I convinced myself Jewel would be strolling in the house at least by midnight. Unfortunately, I was wrong. I paced around the house until one in the morning with no sign of her.

Chapter 13

Lisa

"I'm Watching You"

I knew Touch was bound to fuck up and I would be there to catch his ass. After my embarrassment at the courthouse, I was determined to get this selfish motherfucker. So many nights I'd sat and watch him stagger his drunk ass into the house. This particular night I was hoping I would be just as lucky. My confidence was high, and I was ready to serve up some retribution. If things went as planned, I would follow right behind him and enter his house with ease. I had been playing it low for a while, so I knew his guard would be down.

I was dressed in all black with a hoodie on, and I'd been sitting outside Touch's house for hours waiting for him to come home. I felt like a real gangster as I used binoculars to get a bird's-eye view of his house. Since I didn't know how long I would be waiting, I drank no liquids at all. I was craving some water or a tasty appletini. My mouth was dry as shit. I refused to leave my post, no matter the situation. I even put on Depend underwear, just in case I had to pee, but the lack of fluids in my body prevented me from having to piss myself.

"Finally," I whispered as Touch pulled up in the driveway. I slouched down lower in my seat to shield myself from his eyes.

To my surprise, his guard wasn't down at all. That fool was looking all around under the car, in bushes, and even behind the garbage can, all the while carrying a gun in one hand and talking on his cell phone in another.

My window was down, so I was able to listen closely as he secured the premises before walking in the house. From what I was able to gather, he was leaving Jewel a voice message. He had his beg game on, so I guess Jewel had left him. I laughed to myself and waddled in joy with this newfound discovery. *Karma is a bitch, muthafucka.*

I sat patiently and waited another hour before I attempted to walk into Touch's house. The Touch I knew always hit the blunt and drank a couple shots of Hennessy after a long day. This was the little extra edge I needed before making my move. I quietly climbed out my car and walked to the back door. I turned the knob. This shit was easier than I thought. Touch dumb ass had left the back door unlocked.

"Jewel, is that you?" he called out as I walked through the door.

Shit, I thought to myself knowing for sure I was caught. I froze in my steps, not knowing what to do.

"Jewel? Baby, answer me," Touch shouted out again.

With no other option, I cleared my throat and tried my best to disguise my voice. "Yes, baby," I replied.

"Make me a drink, and bring it in here when you come please, baby," Touch begged.

"Okay."

I grabbed a shot glass and sprinkled a drug called Thorazine in it and mixed it with the Hennessy. I'd learned from a criminal-ass friend of mine that it paralyzes the body. I walked up behind him and put the glass to his lips, and he drank it all down in one big gulp.

"I knew you would come back," he said, slurring his words.

Touch was so drunk, he didn't even notice as I pulled out the rope from my backpack and started wrapping him with it.

"I love you," I whispered in a sweet tone as I knew Jewel probably would. Then I pulled the rope tight.

Touch finally opened his eyes. He began to tussle a bit, but it was too late. The medicine had all ready kicked in.

"What the fuck," were the last words he spoke before I stuck it to him hard, like a virgin with no lubrication.

I pulled out a pair of brass knuckles from my pocket and started beating him with no remorse. I couldn't resist fucking with his manhood, so I stomped on his dick. And to wrap it all up, I knocked out one of his teeth. I was sure to leave my mark, just as he'd done to me. To fuck up his mind even more, I ransacked the place to make it seem like I was looking for something. Satisfied with my handiwork, I took one last look around the place. I figured, since I had the run of the house, I would take something as a memento. I deserved it, considering what Touch had put me through.

I quickly snatched up an iPod from the end table and put it in my pocket. Then I went through Touch's pockets and took all his cash.

My last stop was the kitchen. I opened the refrigerator took out a beer and calmly sat and drank it. Now that my mouth had some saliva back, I went back to Touch and spat in his face before walking out the back door.

Chapter 14

Jewel

"Girl Talk"

Shakira and I spent the morning at Tyson Corner, a mall in Alexandria, Virginia. Our first stop was the M•A•C counter. I could have used some more M•A•C makeup, but I simply couldn't afford it. No Touch meant no money. It was times like these that I hated myself for depending on a man for so long to provide for me. Shakira offered to pay for some items for me in the store, but I refused. She had a little daughter to take care of, and there was no way I would allow her to spend her hard-earned money on me. Besides, this was her first bonus check from her job, and I wanted her to only splurge on herself.

While speaking with Shakira about my situation, I realized it was time I made some changes in my life. I didn't know how, but it was time I figured it out. Back in Virginia, being with Touch was stressful. Not only did I have to put up with his erratic behavior, I had constant irritable bowel syndrome. My stomach was always churning for the worse.

While in DC, I didn't feel the churn at all. I felt re-laxed. Everything felt easier. Also, there was no looking over my shoulder and wondering if someone was go-ing to kill me or him first. Some nights, I would catch Touch looking out the window with his gun in hand, waiting and willing to kill anything that moved. I knew this was the life I chose, but it wasn't the way I wanted to live. Now it was time I broke free. I was truly get-ting too old for the bullshit. Ten years down the road, I didn't want to look back and regret that I'd never made a change for the better.

From the time I reached DC, I'd had my phone turned off, so Touch had no way to contact me. I wanted to be free from the drama, hurt, and pain. To be honest, I had no idea what my next move was, but I was sure it would be a positive one.

Looking at Shakira made me realize what potential I had. I knew if she could do it, I could too. We'd come from the same past and walked the same paths in life.

After browsing the mall a couple of hours, I ended up purchasing a pair of shoes on clearance. For lunch, we went to the Cheesecake Factory. Thankfully, I had a gift card I'd received from my father for my birthday. The total I'd spent for the entire mall day was only thirty dollars and fifteen cents. Being accustomed to spend-ing whatever I wanted, this was a big accomplishment for me, and I couldn't have felt better.

Later that afternoon, we took Shakira's five-year-old daughter, Kelly, to the zoo. It had been years since I was at a zoo, and I was just as excited as Kelly. I always found the animals so exotic and fascinating.

"What flavor snow cone would you like?" I asked Kelly as we walked up to the concession stand. I had a crazy craving for rainbow cotton candy myself.

"Grape, please," she said with a head nod.

"Sure thing!" I smiled as I ran my fingers through Kelly's long, wavy hair. I wondered if my daughter would have such characteristics. Being around Kelly made me second-guess my life decisions and reassess my priorities. I wondered if I had made different decisions in my life if I would've had a child now. I wanted a baby now, so I could raise it to be a respectful, contributing member of society. I became a little sad thinking that I may never have a child.

Shakira had raised Kelly well and taught her respect at a young age. My eyes filled with tears when I observed the loving bond they shared. The most touching time was bedtime. Shakira would bathe Kelly, and after reading her a bedtime story, they both would get on their knees on the side of the bed and say their prayers together.

I couldn't help but think about what it would be like for Touch and I to raise a family together. My thoughts would start out nice enough. Then I would get a vision of Touch walking around with a gun near my baby, and those happy visions would turn into a nightmare.

When the night hit, it was girl time. Shakira called over a neighbor to babysit Kelly, and we hit the road.

"So what's the going rate for a babysitter these days?" I attempted to start a little small talk after being seated. We were dining at Tuna, a local upscale seafood restaurant.

Girl, I don't know. As long as I continue to reload Suzie's iPod gift card and pay her twenty dollars in cash, she's good for the night."

We both started laughing.

"Shakira, I'm proud of you," I had to admit.

"Me?" Shakira said in a surprised tone. "For what?"

"Well, you have got your own place. Your daughter is healthy and happy. You make your own money, and you don't have to depend on a man. All the things I dreamed of."

"Thank you, Jewel." Shakira said, tears in her eyes. She then rose from the table to give me a hug.

"Shakira," I said, surprised at her reaction.

"I really appreciate that, Jewel. You have no idea what that means to me." Shakira wiped the tears from her eyes. "It wasn't easy. A few years ago, I wanted a change from the drug life. I went back to school to become a dental hygienist, and with the help of God, I landed a job right away. Life is all about balance. I've got my Kelly and my job. We are taking it day by day," Shakira explained, looking over at the bar.

"You deserve to be happy," I replied, thinking back to the rough past Shakira had. She was heavy in the drug game because of some shady guys she'd dated, and in order to survive she had to strip.

"And so do you too."

"Sometimes I'm not so sure if I do. I made my bed, and now I have to lay in it," I said, full of self-pity.

"That is not true, Jewel. You control your destiny. You have got to find yourself. Let go of the self-pity and bring that confident, outgoing Jewel I know!"

"I guess you're right. I have sort of lost myself. I've gotta find me and find my happiness in the process. Touch has put me through so much. The fights, the cheating, the mental and physical abuse, and prison have all taken a toll on me. If I told you everything that has happened, you would lose your appetite." I began to tear up. "You know what? The pity stops here. I'm not looking back. I want to look forward from this point on. You're going to be my inspiration." I was fighting to hold back my tears.

"I believe you will change your life." Shakira then hugged me again.

"Yes, I will," I replied, hugging her tight.

"Wow!" Shakira said as she looked toward the bar. "I had no idea dinner was gonna be so emotional!" She gave a grin but seemed a little distracted.

"Shakira, you have been looking at the bar many times. What's up? Is a cutie over there or something?" I asked, no longer able to ignore her constant glares over at the bar.

"Turn around," she said.

I quickly turned around and scanned the entire bar, but the only thing I noticed was the bartender making a flaming drink.

"There, walking out the door."

"Who?" I inquired.

"A woman dressed in jeans and a black sweater. She had a haircut similar to Halle Berry. She was dark-skinned and kept staring in your face the entire time she was on her cell phone," Shakira explained.

"Hhhmm. I don't know anyone that fits that description. Plus, I don't know anyone in this area. Are you sure she wasn't looking at you?"

"No. She was definitely looking at you. Maybe it was a mistaken identity and once she realized you weren't the person, she left."

We both blew it off and left the conversation at that as we enjoyed the rest of our dinner.

As we walked out of the restaurant, I patted my stomach. "Girl, I'm stuffed. That was some good eating." Normally in Virginia my stomach would be doing backflips after a meal like that. Not now though. I was feeling good.

"Yes, I'm stuffed too. The food was so tasty. We have to come here more often." Shakira nodded.

"Where to now?" I asked, yawning.

"Are you tired? I see you yawning."

"No, the night is just getting started for me. Give me thirty minutes, and I will perk back up. The food has got me sleepy. I have a small case of the *itis*." I giggled.

"Well, I want to take you to a place called Pink Dices, a new club in the area. I've heard nothing but good reviews. Plus, if you get in before eleven, ladies get a free drink."

"I'm in! I need a drink, and I love free!" I laughed, giving Shakira a high-five.

"Jewel," a voice called out behind me.

Shakira and I both turned around wondering who the hell would know me in DC. But when we looked around, there was no one else in the parking lot. I began to develop goose bumps. Both of us wanted nothing else but to get the hell up out of there. Chills went down my spine as I wondered, *Did Touch send someone to spy on me? Has he found me?*

Shakira and I darted out of the parking lot. I was so shaken up, I didn't feel like going out after all. My stomach got that queasy feeling I would get back home. My night was ruined by Touch once again. Would I ever be able to live a stress-free life?

Chapter 15

Unknown Person

"Unveiling the Truth"

I hope Jewel didn't see me last night, I thought as I got out of my car. I knew it was likely that she may have seen me because I couldn't stop staring at her. I just couldn't help myself. She was just so beautiful, much prettier than I'd remembered. I wish I could have approached her that night, but the time wasn't right. I needed some time to gather my thoughts and figure out what I wanted to say to her. I was sure that other chick she was with caught a glimpse of me, and she was making my spot hot. That's why I had to dip out so quickly.

Finding Jewel had been much easier than I had anticipated. The first thing I did was to go to all of her known addresses. She obviously was at none of them. Next, I checked the prison and court records to see if I could find anything out. I saw that her case had been dismissed, and there was no record of her being in prison. So I knew she was still on the outside.

The last thing I did was put a trace on her cell phone. Being an undercover cop, I had associated with many underground types, and the one I needed at the moment was a master computer hacker. He went by the nickname CyberRat because he said he could root around and find any information you needed. It was not even a day before CyberRat came back to me with a general location for Jewel, and more information than I had asked for. He had hacked into her e-mails and found some information pertaining to her looking for employment. I knew this information was going to come in handy. I packed up a suitcase and was headed for DC an hour after I received the information.

Being a cop on a stakeout was one thing, but being a stalker was on a whole other level. I'd made arrangements for Jewel to come into the bookstore, Barnes and Noble, to meet a person named Joel. Because I had access to her e-mails I had replied to her, acting as a potential employer. She answered, and we agreed to meet for an interview. Little did she know, I'd been pretending to be this Joel guy the entire time.

I knew Jewel was about her dollars, and from the sound of her e-mails, her money was getting scarce, so I played on that. I sent her an e-mail guaranteeing her fast money with little risk. I knew it would sound too good for her to pass up.

As soon as I walked in the store, I spotted Jewel sitting at a table in the café. I had come a little early, so I could pick the perfect spot and relax a bit before approaching her, but that plan was out the door. Jewel must have been real hungry for cash to show up this early. Normally, with her attitude and ego, she would show up late, to prove she was in charge.

Seeing her there already threw me off my game. I almost turned around and walked right back out, but

I convinced myself to stay. The opportunity had finally come for me to confess my love. It was what kept me going when I was at my lowest point. I took a deep breath in and walked over to Jewel. I was nervous, and my stomach was turning upside down as I approached her.

"Jewel," I carefully greeted her. She was taking a peek at the latest *Cosmo* magazine.

"Misty?" she responded, taking off her sunglasses. "What the fuck is this?"

"May I please sit down?" I asked, expecting her to decline and possibly even smack me in my face. If she declined, I was already prepared to beg her to listen.

"What the fuck? I thought you was dead?"

"I'm not. It's really me. The force just made that up to try and get rid of me. I've been thinking of you for so long." My eyes watered. I was so happy to speak with her. She hadn't ran off or slapped me. I was hopeful that she felt the same way about me as I felt about her.

"Are you fuckin' serious? Fuck that! Get the hell away from me! You come into my life to get me set up with the feds, and I'm just supposed to fuckin' welcome you back? When I saw your face flash on the news with the words, 'Officer killed in the line of duty,' I was happy that shit happened to you. All the shit I told you, all the times I spilled my guts to my caring nurse, when the whole time you was a fuckin' cop! I trusted you, bitch! You were my best fuckin' friend!" Jewel shouted then stormed off.

I took a deep breath and prayed that the words coming out of my mouth would make her listen to me. "Give me five minutes. That's it. I won't bother you again. Please, Jewel, I'm begging you." I followed behind her.

Jewel turned around, and I braced myself for a smack to the face, but to my surprise, she said, "You got three fuckin' minutes. Don't waste my time. You've stolen enough of my life already!"

"Well, um—" I began to stutter, but Jewel cut me off.

"Oh, and let me guess—You're Joel. Me trying to make some money was a smokescreen for you. What a fuckin' asshole! Wow, look at the time. I've talked for one of your three minutes. You better hurry up. You may proceed now," she said, looking at her watch.

I took another deep breath. "You need to know that I have loved you since the first time I saw you. You were lying there in the hospital, and you looked so beautiful even in such a fragile state. It may sound cliché as hell, but it's the truth. I got kicked off the case for you. My colleagues had a hunch I was tampering with evidence to protect you, and they were right. I'll do anything for you. I was offered a desk job, but I turned it down after getting hurt. The bottom line, I've been suspended until further notice."

Jewel shook her head. "This isn't making sense to me."

"Jewel, I was tampering with evidence so the heat could come off you."

"What?"

"I couldn't have you doing prison time. I was never going to testify against you or bring evidence that would lead to a conviction because I couldn't bear the fact that it would split us apart. I was falling in love with you. I am in love with you. I risked everything for you. The force is all I had. It was my daily motivation, and I lived to work undercover. Since it's been gone,

I've had a chance to realize there is a life outside of that. You're the only thing I've ever loved, other than being an agent. And that's why I'm here today. I need you in my life."

"So are the police still watching us?"

"Yes," I answered honestly. "That's why they faked my death. Touch and you had to believe I was dead so that they could continue their case. The force felt that you guys would get relaxed and feel like your case was open and shut, and soon let your guards down."

"Wow!" She looked off into space.

"Although I'm not on the force anymore, I still have a few friends that keep me in the loop. I refuse to let you get wrapped up in Touch's shit. The best thing you could have done was move out. You need to stay away from him. They want Touch so bad."

"You've lied before, former best friend," Jewel said. "So how do I know you're not lying to me right now? Why should I trust you?"

"Jewel, I love you," I simply stated.

"This is a lot to take in. You've deceived me once. I don't know if I could ever forgive you. I didn't even know you were gay."

"All the signs were there. You just didn't want to notice. After getting hurt, I was placed in physical therapy, and to get through the pain, all I did was think about you giving me another chance. No more lies and deceit, Jewel, I promise. I'm standing here asking for forgiveness."

"I gotta go," Jewel said.

It was obvious she couldn't take anymore. It was just too much for her.

"Can I at least give you my number, and maybe you can call me some time?" I asked with my best puppy-dog face.

"I guess," she responded, pulling out her cell phone.

This was definitely a good start, better than I'd ever expected. I walked out of the store a happy camper. As soon as I got in my car, my cell phone rang. I pressed talk without even looking at the number, excited that Jewel had decided to call right away. I was hoping she had decided to grab a bite to eat and talk about things.

"Hello," I said right away, expecting to hear Jewel's voice on the other end.

"Hey, baby," a voice said.

I took the phone away from my ear and looked at the caller ID. That definitely wasn't Jewel's voice. The caller ID said Jamie.

"Hello?" Jamie said in response to my moment of silence.

"Hey, Jamie. How are you?" I said, a little disappointed that it was him instead of Jewel.

"I'm good. Missing you."

"Awww! How sweet! I'm in the middle of something right now. Can I call you back in a few?" I said, rushing to get Jamie off the phone.

"Sure. No problem," he said before hanging up.

I really wasn't feeling Jamie, or any man for that matter. Since my time in rehab, I had come to terms with the fact that I was a lesbian. I knew, deep down inside, the other night with Jamie was a big mistake. It was a moment of weakness, a test to see if I was really gay. The only good thing that came out of it was, it confirmed my love for Jewel, and that I definitely liked women. I should have never fooled around with him. He'd just caught me at a vulnerable moment. Somehow I had to get Jamie out my life and Jewel in it. I wasn't sure how I was going to do it, but it had to happen.

I pondered this dilemma all the way back to Virginia. I'd driven all the way from Virginia Beach just to meet with Jewel. As I drove, I thought long and hard about my feelings for Jamie and my feelings for Jewel. No matter from which angle I looked at things, it always pointed back at Jewel. For some reason, I just couldn't let her slip through my fingers again.

By the time I'd hit Seven Cities, my mind was made up. I had to get rid of Jamie. I saw no upside to keeping him in my life.

Chapter 16

Touch

"Does Someone Have Voodoo on Me?"

In all my years of being in the drug game, I ain't never had no fucking body come where I lay my head at and put their hands on me. This is some bullshit, I thought to myself as I looked over my numerous scars and my missing tooth in the bathroom mirror.

I couldn't believe that shit had really happened to me. The fucked-up thing about it, I couldn't remember a gotdamn thing about the previous night. I was seriously going to have to consider not getting so fucked up on booze and weed. What I did know was, it had to be a nigga to do that shit. Sure, I thought about that psycho Lisa, but there was no way that bitch would have the strength to tie me up.

I wracked my brain trying to figure out who the fuck it could have been. I ain't had no beef on the streets, so it wasn't from a business associate. *Maybe it was Lisa and some nigga that did this to me,* I thought as I prepared to hit the road. If so, that bitch was reaching new levels of crazy, and I would need to end her life for that shit.

I was headed straight to the dentist. There was no way in hell I was walking around town looking like a fucking crackhead with missing teeth. As I got dressed, I continued to think through all the people it might be that fucked me up. That's when that nigga Rico popped in my head. All of a sudden, he'd moved to the top of my list of suspects. If it wasn't for Jewel's dumb ass inviting him into my house, the other night probably would have never happened. If the bitch was so eager to fuck, why couldn't she fuck him at his house?

Fuming from the thoughts of this nigga fucking me up like he did, I called Jewel up. I wanted her to know that she was going to be responsible for this nigga's death. I got her voice mail. I called back to back three more times and got her voice mail every time. The last time, I decided to leave a message.

"Jewel, you know who the hell this is. Answer the phone when I call you. Your boyfriend paid me a visit. You should have said your final good-byes the last time you saw him because he's dead for sure now!" I screamed in the phone.

I was hoping that message would get her attention. I went to take a leak, and before I could finish the phone was ringing. I knew it was Jewel. I answered right away ready to light her ass up.

"Yo', bitch, you got it coming to you when I see you," I yelled into the phone as soon as I picked up.

"Yo', nigga, this Deuce. What's up with you? Long night last night?" Deuce laughed.

What the fuck he mean by that? Is he referring to me getting a beat-down? Is he involved?

Many thoughts went streaming through my mind. Now I had another suspect to consider. The last thing I wanted to do was to off this nigga. It could cause some major problems with Jimmy and me. Which would seriously affect my money. I didn't even bother explaining my situation with that nigga. We had a brief business talk, and I got off the phone.

Despite the bullshit I was going through, I had to get on with my day. I hopped in my truck and started out the neighborhood. I didn't even get to the end of the block before it shut off on me.

"Damn!" I banged the steering wheel then got out.

I had to wonder if this day could get any worse. Thinking maybe it was the battery, I popped the hood. When I got out of the truck, I noticed my gas tank was open with a little note tied to it. The note read, "Sweeter than sugar, baby."

"Damn it!" I yelled to no one in particular.

Just when I thought it was over, Lisa struck again. *This bitch is relentless,* I thought. I looked down at my ringing cell phone. It was Jimmy.

"Hey, Jimmy. What's up?" I greeted him, trying to maintain my composure on the phone.

"There is a slight problem with our pictures," he said, letting me know there was a problem with the business.

"From my end, there isn't a problem. The pictures seem clear to me. Everything is accounted for," I said, assuring Jimmy that all the figures added up.

"I will be home soon to straighten it out."

"All right. So everything good otherwise?" I asked.

"See you soon," Jimmy responded, cutting me off, and hung up the phone.

I could tell by that conversation that things weren't good. I wasn't too worried because I knew I made sure everything was accounted for at all times. I wasn't no rookie to the game, so I knew to not even be a dollar short when working on consignment. Having Jimmy back on the street was going to be nice. I couldn't wait for his release.

I called up ma dukes to take me to the dentist. I had to get my grill right, but after that, it was pure relaxation. I looked forward to locking myself in the house and drinking a few Heinekens, smoking a blunt, while watching my DVD collection of *Martin*. I had to do something to keep from catching a murder charge. I didn't know if it would be that bitch Lisa or that punk Rico, but somebody was gonna die soon.

Chapter 17

Jewel

"Making a Change"

I finally mustered up the energy to listen to the numerous voice mails Touch had left. I already had an idea what to look forward to. *Bitch* was my middle name to him if he was angry.

Touch barked on the phone, *"Bitch, I know you were behind this. Don't worry. We'll get another battle together. This time, I will be the only one standing. I thought you learned your lesson last time I beat your ass. Sending that nigga to my fuckin' house. Is you crazy?"*

The next few messages after that started off the same way, "Bitch this, bitch that." *Here we go again,* I thought. Others messages followed, but they were kind and sweet, with Touch damn near begging me to come back to him. Blah, blah, blah, it was all the same shit with Touch—Yell at me, hit me then proclaim how sorry you are and how much you love me. I deleted the messages. I was really starting to tire of his stupid ass. I thought about calling him and chewing his ass out, but I dialed another number instead. Without giving it a second thought, I pressed send.

"Hello," I heard on the other end of the phone.

Although I wanted to speak, no words came out. I didn't really have a reason to call. I was just feeling lonely and wanted someone to talk to. It didn't hurt that I had been intrigued by Misty's offer ever since we'd met at the bookstore café.

"Hello?" the voice said again.

"Hi." I managed to force out one word.

"Jewel?" Misty sounded excited.

"Yes. I had no one else to call."

"Hey, baby. I'm so happy you called. I never thought I would see this day. I'm here for you. What's on your mind?"

"Just going through the highs and lows of Touch. I just checked my voice messages, and it was the same old thing I have been dealing with. It seemed like every other word was *bitch*. Men don't understand how much that word really hurts. I guess they were going-away presents."

"That's crazy. Jewel, I told you, you deserve better. No man should ever disrespect you like that," Misty said, a bit of anger in her tone.

"Plus, he fucked some girl name Lisa and end up beating her or something. They went to court, and he won the case, and now she's out for revenge. This chick came to my house and everything. It was a mess."

"He cheats on you, and now Lisa won't go away. Jewel, this is crazy. I can't believe you are even keeping contact with him. Why don't you get a new phone? I'll pay for it." She sounded so soothing.

"You know how hard it was to hold my composure when Touch told me he had to go to court behind her?"

"I can tell you're still hurting behind all of this. Sounds like you're getting angry all over again just talking about it."

"You're probably right. I feel like a hole has been ripped through my heart. I don't know what to do. I thought he was my best friend, but friends don't treat each other like this, do they?"

"No, Jewel, they don't. My best advice to you is to separate yourself from him. It's the only way you will get strong, independent, and feel more secure about yourself. What can I do to help you? I am here for you, no matter what."

"You're right. It's time to make a change. Thanks for talking to me, Misty. I really need an ear to listen. You always were a good listener, even if it was to try and get information for the feds."

"I am so sorry about all of that, Jewel. Even though I was trying to put Touch away, I would never have hurt you. It seemed like I was interested in what you had to say, because I was. I still am. You are an amazing and beautiful woman."

Misty's sincerity made me cry. No one had been this kind to me in a long while. All the stress of my life with Touch was coming out through those tears.

"Thanks, Misty. You are too kind. I have to be going now. You've given me a lot to think about," I said, wiping my tears.

I was glad I'd called Misty. It felt like the best decision I had made in a while. I found comfort in talking with her. It felt familiar. Before I knew she was a cop, when we would have our conversations, I'd always appreciated her advice. She was so confident and knew the answer to everything. She always seemed to know what to say, and at the right time. Once again I found myself putting my trust in Misty. I prayed to God I wasn't making a horrible mistake like I'd done in the past.

After talking to Misty, it was clear that I needed to go back to Virginia and face my demons once and for all. I started by calling my lawyer and telling him I needed an appointment to come in and talk to him about my case. Then I called a moving company and my real estate agent. Once everything was in order, I planned to hit the road the next morning.

I woke up the next morning optimistic. I knew I was making the right decision. I said my good-byes to Shakira before leaving. She was a good friend, and I was grateful for her kindness. She was definitely one of a kind, and I felt I would always be indebted to her for accepting me with open arms.

"Good luck today. Hope everything goes as planned," Shakira said, giving me a big hug.

I didn't want to let go. One part of me was excited to face my past and move on, and the other was scared to death of the unknown.

"I'm sure it will," I assured her as we walked toward the door.

I loaded my car with my luggage then I hopped in. I waved a final good-bye as I drove off.

"Drive safe," Shakira yelled as I pulled off.

Attempting to beat the traffic, I left DC close to six o'clock in the morning. I put on the tune of Nicki Minaj to keep me energized. It seemed like I got to the Tidewater area in no time at all. As I drove through the

Hampton tunnel I began to get nervous. My legs were shaking as reality set in. I didn't know if I was truly ready to face my past, but in order for me to have a brighter future, I knew I had to.

My first stop was Norfolk to meet with my lawyer, Eric Dickerson. I told him everything Misty had shared with me. He was grateful for the information but warned me to stand clear of Misty. He thought she may have ulterior motives and not truly there to protect me. I heard what he was saying, but in my heart I felt Misty's motives were sincere. Call me stupid, but I believed her. I trusted her more than I trusted Touch. Touch always vowed he would never do a long bid ever again. Plus, his motto was money over bitches, so why wouldn't he sell me out to stay on the streets and make money?

Based on what I shared with Mr. Dickerson, he made a deal with the DA's office. In exchange for my testimony, I would receive immunity. Besides, Touch was the one the city of Virginia Beach and feds truly wanted, not me. I was just a pawn. Touch would do the same to me. *Fuck him. I'll get him before he gets me. This is the new Jewel. I ain't no ride-or-die no more. It's about taking care of myself.*

"Thanks for signing on the dotted line. My office will be in touch," the district attorney said with a smile on his face after receiving my written statement. I'd written a three-page testimony about what was really going down. Which was enough to put Touch away for a long while. Oh well, serves his ass right.

On my way to my next task I felt conflicted about agreeing to testify against Touch. Yes, I was mad at him, but did that warrant me helping to put him in jail? There were some good things about him. I truly feel that he did love me, and if I had to be truthful with myself, I did love him. I had to ask myself if my love outweighed the anxiety and heartbreak he caused me. I started having second thoughts about my decision to testify. I thought about different ways I might be able to move on, but I saw none. Touch would never let me be at peace. If I wanted a clean break and a fresh start, I had to testify. It was all about me now.

When I pulled up in front of my house, the moving company already had their men and truck waiting out front. With precision and laser-like speed, they moved everything to a storage unit, except for Touch's belongings. I had them move all of Touch's things to the garage. I wasn't so cold-hearted that I would throw all his stuff away. He would have the opportunity to collect his belongings if he wanted. I still had some guilt about my impending testimony. After changing the locks, the garage would be all he had access to. Lucky for him, I didn't reprogram the garage opener as well.

The real estate agent was right on time with the contract and for sale sign for the house. I was going to sell it as is. I had no time or money to fix the house up, and I wasn't really looking for a huge profit. I just wanted all links to Virginia and Touch severed, and that house was the last thing tying me to either of them.

By the end of the day, I was exhausted, but I felt free as a bird. Little by little, I was lifting the burden and weight I had been carrying on my back.

I checked myself into a local hotel for the night. I had planned to head back to DC in the morning. Shakira had agreed to let me stay with her until I was able to get things sorted out. I lay my head down to sleep and vowed to myself that Touch will never have the opportunity to disrespect me again. No more name-calling, no more cheating, and no more physical and mental abuse. I knew I didn't deserve any of that, and I refused to take his shit anymore.

As I lay my head on the pillow and thought about my future, I had a huge smile on my face. Independence suited me well. I was excited about my new beginning.

Chapter 18

Touch

"Looking for a Pick-me-up"

"We had shit rolling tonight, man," Deuce said as we wrapped things up. It seemed like every day business was increasing. The fiends were getting word that we had the best shit in Virginia.

Business was going so well, I had spent the weekend at the spot. I didn't want to take the chance of a nigga fucking up or attempting to pull some old "I got robbed" bullshit. I stayed around to set an example for the young niggas. Show them how a real businessman conducts himself. The blocks we had on lock in Norfolk were definitely paying off.

"Knowing the right people and having good product shows in our profits," I stated as I counted up the last stack of money, verifying it was accurate.

"You right about that. Get some rest. I'm about to do the same." Deuce grabbed the money stacks and put them in the duffle bag.

"I can't wait to lay my head down either," I said as I gathered my things.

I hadn't had a bath or even brushed my teeth the entire weekend. It was like a conveyor belt of fiends coming through the door. I barely had time to breathe. I couldn't wait to get home, get a hot shower, and lay it down in my bed. Of course, I was going to need to smoke some weed before all that.

I stopped at the door and turned toward Deuce before leaving. "Did you need me to do the drop for Jimmy?" I asked.

"Nah, man. Have a good one," he replied, grabbing the duffle bag and heading toward the door behind me.

I hopped in my truck, eager to get home. One of them cats around the way who used to be in the drug game had taken my truck over the weekend and fixed that shit. Lucky for me, he was a good-ass mechanic and was able to get it running again. I was tired as hell and happy that I didn't have to call a cab. On my way home, I started thinking about ways I could use all of the cash coming my way. I needed to set up some sort of legit business to protect my ass from prosecution.

The longer Jewel was away, the more I got used to not having her around. Don't get me wrong. I still needed her in my life, but it was getting easier to deal with. I decided to call Jewel when I got back to the crib and try one more time to get her back home.

When I entered the garage, I noticed a number of boxes stacked up in the corner. Being extra cautious, I pulled my gun and looked around to see if whoever stacked the boxes was still lingering. This shit looked suspicious. After getting out the car, I walked to the boxes. Each one had my name written on it with a black marker. I cautiously opened one box and looked through it. It had my underwear and some T-shirts in it. I started opening each box, and each one contained my possessions. All my shit had been thrown into boxes and put in the garage. It didn't take me long to figure what was going on.

Right away I assumed Jewel was back home and was trying to make some statement. I stormed toward the house. I tried opening the door from the garage, but my key didn't work. So I stomped out the garage door toward the front yard and noticed a for sale sign on the front lawn. That's when it hit me like a fucking freight train! Not only was Jewel making a point and getting rid of my stuff, she was selling the house right up from under me. That bitch had some nerve, especially since I'd paid for the house! That's the fucked-up part about the drug game. You have the money but can't put shit in your name. I'd never thought Jewel would do some shit like that to me.

This new drama gave me an extra boost of energy. Now I was even more determined to get some sort of legit business going. I dialed Jewel's number, this time to let her know she won. I was laying my flag down. I couldn't handle this bullshit no more. There were plenty of bitches out there happy to be my girl. But when I called, I got a recording stating her number was no longer in service. Jewel had changed her number on me. It was at that point I realized she was serious. There was no turning back for either of us. Now I would have to fight her for custody of my child.

I dug through the boxes and found some clothes to last me a few days. I checked in a hotel, got a quick shower, then took a little nap.

After my rest, I was rejuvenated, so I hit a local lounge I used to frequent named Mo Dean's. My episode earlier had me wanting to take out some aggression on some pussy. A halo of smoke greeted me at the door. There were a couple of guys playing pool, but the majority of the people seemed to be watching the game on the flat-screen televisions placed throughout the bar. It was a big playoff game on, and the place was packed with screaming fans. I really wasn't in the mood for a large crowd, but I wasn't about to sit up in a hotel room thinking about all the fucked-up things that had happened in the past few days.

I found a seat in the corner and began to watch the game as I waited for a waitress to come over and take my drink order. Out of the corner of my right eye, I noticed a cutie named Diana I had dealt with in the past. She was heading over in my direction. My dick got hard almost instantly as I thought back to the good times I had with her. She was a freak in bed, and because of it she was given the nickname Dirty Diana.

"A Grey Goose on the rocks," she said as soon as she walked up.

"So you remember, huh?" I laughed. Back in the day when I used to frequent this bar, that was my drink, and Diana was my favorite waitress.

"That's not all I remember. You know I ain't working tonight." Diana grabbed my hand and placed it between her legs.

Damn! Some things never change, I thought. Dirty Diana was still the freak I'd fucked over a year ago.

I said straight up, "It's been a long time. You gonna give me some of that?" There was no need trying to be a gentleman with this bitch.

"Follow me," she instructed, motioning with her finger.

She led me to the bathroom hardly anyone uses in the back. As soon as we entered the stall, Diana began unbuttoning her blouse. With her shirt and bra completely open, she started massaging my dick back and forth with her hands.

"Damn, girl! I like that."

"Come take this pussy, it's yours," she said while placing my hand in her pants.

"I could get into that, but first, you know what I like," I said caressing her face.

"All you had to do was say the word," Diana replied unbuttoning my jeans and letting down the zipper.

That's what I loved about Diana. She got down to the business, with no questions asked. It took this girl no time to whip my dick out and put it into her mouth. She didn't start slow but worked right into deep-throating it. My eyes were rolling in the back of my head. Then Diana jerked me off while sucking my balls. A minute later she went right back to the deep throat. I had to admit, this girl gave the best head of all time.

She suddenly stopped, knowing I was close to coming. "It's time for some pussy," she whispered in my ear.

"We got plenty of time for that when I take you home. Diana, come on now, finish sucking me off. You the best," I said, motioning for her head to come to my dick.

When I came, that girl swallowed every drop. She drained me to the point where I couldn't move. After that I definitely needed a drink. We headed back to the table, and I ordered a Rémy straight.

Chapter 19

Lisa

"Sweet, Sweet Revenge"

Getting revenge on Touch was becoming more like a job. My drive for revenge had turned into damn near stalking him. I considered installing a surveillance camera in the kitchen and the living room of his house when I beat his ass, but I figured it was too risky. I'd spent days driving past his house and sometimes waiting for hours for him to arrive. But I still couldn't get down a system as to his schedule. He never seemed to stick to a pattern. I did notice that before getting out of the car, he made sure his gun was in his hand and cocked. I wasn't taking no chances with that. I knew I would surely end up dead if I tried to ambush him as he arrived home.

For one night I had decided to take a night off and focus on me. It was time I got my mind off Touch and moved on to the next man. I knew I couldn't stalk him forever, but I was having so much fun doing it, I didn't really want to stop just yet. I'd already dedicated too much of my life to Touch, so what was a few more days. I was there before Jewel, dealing with the baby momma drama and all his bullshit. Then we broke up, and he came back, and I accepted him, and we ended up in court. I guess I should have followed the rule, "Never go back." Well, it was definitely time to move forward, and I wanted and needed some positive attention from a man.

A quick trip to MacArthur Center led me to a BeBe dress with a one-hundred-and-sixty-five-dollar price tag. The original price was two hundred, but my girl who worked there let me use her employee discount. This dress was definitely going to get me the attention I was so craving. It had been weeks since I rode a dick or hung out with my girls, and I was looking forward to doing both.

When I got home I grabbed a bite to eat and relaxed a little before my big night. My relaxation turned into a nap. When I woke up, I took a quick glimpse at the clock. It was eleven o'clock. I was surely going to be late, since I was supposed to meet my girls in a half hour. Now they would get first dibs on all the fine brothers up in the bar.

"Damn it!" I yelled to no one particular.

I jumped up and rushed to the shower. I was planning to meet my girls at Mo Dean's Restaurant and Lounge, a well-known spot in Norfolk where all the ballers hung out.

By twelve I was pulling up in the parking lot. I rushed inside the bar to meet my girls, who were already there waiting on me. I found them right away parked at a prime table where all could see them. I greeted everyone and grabbed a seat. I hadn't been sitting five minutes before the waitress walked up.

"Excuse me," the waitress said to me.

"Yes," I replied a little annoyed that I barely had time to settle in and she was already hounding me for my order.

"Here is an apple martini. The gentleman at the bar ordered it for you," she said as she pointed him out. "This is also for you." She handed me a napkin.

I noticed the gentleman's number was written on the elaborate napkin the waitress had just given me. "Thank you," I said smiling. I felt a little stupid for getting an attitude with the waitress.

I then turned to my girls and said, "I guess the expensive-ass dress was worth it!"

"Heeeyyyy," we all said as we toasted to one another.

My girls, Candi and Sharon, were hyped up. I was the first one to get some action from a man that night, and I'd only been in the spot for a few minutes. This man favored the singer and actor, Tyrese. I wasn't going to waste any time heading in his direction. Judging by the mischief in his eyes, I knew this was gonna be a good night, and I was eager to get it started.

"Oh shit," Candi blurted out after I got up out of my seat.

"What, bitch?" I asked in a panic, wondering if I had come on my period and had a big blood spot on my ass.

"Look." Candi pointed to a corner in the bar.

I turned to look where Candi was pointing. Touch was sitting at a table in the corner, and some new bitch was with him. My stomach turned, and my mood changed almost instantly. I thought he'd left me for his soon-to-be baby mother, Jewel. I about near had a conniption fit. The one night I tried to get away from this nigga, he showed up in the same spot I was at. All I wanted tonight was a good time with some big-dick baller, and now Touch had to go and ruin that shit. I just shook my head as I stared daggers at him.

"Lisa, just ignore him. It's all about us having fun," Sharon reminded me, trying her best to get me focused.

"Yeah, you're right." I nodded. At least in my head I knew she was right, but my heart was elsewhere.

I started walking over to the Tyrese look-alike, but I couldn't help myself. I had to make a slight detour and walk over to where Touch was sitting instead. He didn't notice me as I walked up because he was too busy spouting his stupid game, but I was definitely about to make my presence known.

"What up, whore?" I said, startling him.

Touch looked up at me. "Lisa, don't start your bullshit tonight. I'm not in the mood." He shook his head.

I said to the woman that sat beside him, "And you are?"

"Diana." She rolled her neck and stood up in my face. "Who the hell are you?"

"I'm Lisa. I just would like to let you know, Diana, that Touch beat me, stole my car, and ate up my ice cream. You're a pretty girl. Find someone else and get rid of this trash in your life."

Truly, she wasn't that cute, but anybody could've done better than Touch.

Touch got between me and Diana. "Get the fuck out of here!" he screamed.

"Still the same bullshit with you, Touch. I feel like this is déjà vu. This is the same shit that happened the last time we hooked up in the bar. I don't need drama in my life. You know how to find me when you're drama free. I'm just looking for a good time, drama free. Peace." Diana threw him deuces as she walked off.

Touch turned over the table and put his fist in the air as though he was gonna hit me. The bar went completely silent, except for the sound of the televisions.

"Hit me, so I can haul your ass back to jail," I proclaimed. I was scared as hell and didn't want another busted nose, but I refused to punk down to him, especially since I knew the entire bar was watching.

We stood face to face with Touch's fist raised for what seemed like forever. Touch finally lowered his fist when he realized there were witnesses. Instead of hitting me, he spat in my face. With my finger, I wiped the spit off my face and smeared it on his. Touch was enraged. I had just humiliated his ass in front of the whole bar. I was sure this would take him over the edge. I thought I was about to get an ass-whipping of a lifetime.

I took a deep breath and closed my eyes as I waited for the impact of his fist coming across my face. As I heard him growl, I braced my body for the impending impact of fist on face. Then I heard a crash that wasn't bone against bone. I opened one eye to see Touch had punched a hole in the wall. I opened my other eye as he pushed his way through the crowd.

"Fuck you, Lisa!" he yelled as he went through the barroom door.

I rolled my eyes and acted like it was no big deal, but truthfully I was scared. Relieved to have my face intact and needing to regain composure, I immediately headed to the bathroom. While there, I not only washed my face, but I got prepared for all the strange looks I was about to receive when I walked back out. I fixed my hair and makeup, sprayed on some perfume, looked myself in the eyes, and gave myself a pep talk. Holding my head high and poking out my breasts, I strutted out the bathroom like I was walking in a high-end fashion show.

I was surprised at the reaction of everyone at the bar. I didn't notice any strange looks. Most people either avoided eye contact, while some of the girls gave me a pat on my back and said, "You go, girl."

"Stand up for yourself."

"You a bad bitch."

As soon as I walked back to the table, Candi said, "Damn, bitch! You crazy!"

"*O-M-G*, Lisa!" Sharon chimed in. "I can't believe you did that."

My girls wouldn't shut up about how I'd handled Touch. In fact, it was the topic of discussion for the rest of the night.

Deep inside I was ashamed of my actions. I was never that "psycho bitch" kind of girl, but something about Touch just took me there. It was like he added fuel to my fire. His nonchalance toward me and his selfish attitude had me doing things way out of character. Things could have been different, if only he had just given me a genuine sorry for what he had done to me. Then it would have been so much easier for me to just walk away. But no, his dumb ass couldn't see that he used me and didn't have feelings for me at all. He was freeloading off my ass and spending all my hard-earned money. Then he goes and lays hands on me! I mean, really? Who does that?

To make matters worse, he was already involved with another woman and lied about it. He had the nerve to treat me as if I had known there was another chick in the picture from the beginning. We all know if that was the case and I was truly made aware of Jewel, he would have never gotten my pussy. I had never played the number two role.

The rest of the night was spent bitching about men. Each of my girls had their own horror stories to tell. Each of their stories always ended up saying that they wished they had the balls to do what I had done. While they were telling their stories I was in my own world. After my run-in with Touch, I had a feeling that our relationship wasn't going to end pretty. Touch was pissed off, and I wasn't about to give up fucking with him. Something had to give, and I was afraid one of us would end up dead.

Chapter 20

Misty

"Sweet Seduction"

I stopped washing dishes and dried my hands when my cell phone rang. It was Jewel calling. I desperately wanted to answer, but part of me wanted to send her to voice mail. I figured playing some games might make her want me more. I'd been on an emotional roller coaster as of late, and my feelings for her were consuming me. I gave in to my desire for her.

"Hey," I answered.

"I did it," she stated immediately.

"Did what?" I asked.

"I left Touch. I finally got the nerve to do it. I've been with him for so many years, it was hard to break away."

I could tell Jewel was trying to hold back the tears. And I certainly was hoping she was able to do so, because I didn't want her to shed one damn tear over Touch. He wasn't worth it. Although I didn't hear crying, I could still hear the pain in her voice. It broke my heart to hear it, and all I wanted to do was reach through that phone and hold her.

"Jewel, I know it was hard, but I'm proud of you for realizing that you deserve so much better."

"I moved everything out of the house and put it up for sale. It was difficult packing most of the belongings I could travel with in my car and putting the rest in storage, but I knew I had to do it. The realtor agreed to call me first thing if she had an offer on the table for me. The money from the sale of the house will help me finance a new beginning for myself. And you're not gonna believe this. I talked to my attorney and signed a statement telling them all about Touch and the business. They're granting me immunity for my testimony. That was the most difficult decision I'd ever had to make in my life, but it was necessary."

"That was very brave of you, but like you said, it was necessary. In order to move forward, you have to let go of the past," I said.

"You're right. I'm tired of looking in the past. Now, I'm definitely looking forward to the future," Jewel said, sounding upbeat for the first time in our conversation.

"Now that's the confidence I like to hear! So what's the plan?" I inquired.

"Well, my best buddy Shakira and her daughter couldn't be happier knowing I am going to be staying with them for a while. Then as soon as the house is sold, I'm going to look for my own apartment. In the meantime, I'll be looking for a legit way to make some cash."

"Damn! Sounds like you got it all mapped out. So here's another question for you that doesn't require as much planning. What are your plans for tonight?"

"Not much. I'm heading to Shakira's now. Probably get something to eat and then decompress after my stressful day."

"Well, before you head in that direction, would you like to come by for a few drinks and unwind? You can decompress over here. I'll cook you some dinner, and we can hang out a bit."

"Sure," Jewel said right away, surprising me.

"I'm near Crystal City. When we hang up, I'll text you the address. You just let your GPS do the rest."

"Sounds good. I'll see you in a little while," she said.

I quickly ran around my place tidying up. I wanted it to look perfect for Jewel. I was so excited that she had agreed to come over and spend some time with me. I lit scented candles, started preparing the meal, and even had time to take a quick shower. Before I knew it, there was a knock at the door.

"Coming," I yelled as I rushed toward the door. Before opening it I smoothed my hair, took a deep breath, and put a big smile on my face.

"Hi," Jewel greeted me as the door opened. She seemed a little apprehensive and gave me this look as if I better not dare ask for a hug or touch her for that matter.

"Hey." I acted like I didn't notice her look and directed her to the living room area. "Have a seat." I motioned to the sofa.

"Wow! This is really nice," Jewel said, looking around.

"Thanks," I replied as I headed to the kitchen. "You hungry? I haven't eaten anything today."

The aroma of stir fry filled the air. I knew one of Jewel's favorite dishes was shrimp in garlic sauce, but all I had was chicken, so I improvised. I threw the chicken in a skillet.

"Yes, I am, actually," she responded.

The energy in the room was tight, and I could tell her mind was elsewhere. I needed to lighten the mood, so I popped open a bottle of Moscato and pressed play on the DVD player to Martin Lawrence standup show called *You So Crazy*. Jewel hadn't laughed in a long time, and I was hoping a glass of wine and comedy could fix that.

"Thank you," she said as I handed her the glass of wine.

Minutes later as I was putting the finishing touches on dinner, I heard her laughing. Then I served her my beloved chicken stir fry. I kept the wine flowing and the mood light.

It wasn't long before I could see Jewel becoming tipsy. She had gone from uneasy to relaxed and extra giddy in under an hour.

After dinner I took Jewel to the balcony. The cool breeze of the night air was perfect. We looked in into the sky and admired the full moon and countless stars in the sky. I couldn't have painted a more romantic sky. I was feeling relaxed and happy with her.

"Misty, thank you for being there for me. A big dose of laughter and a little pampering was just what I needed." Jewel then downed the last bit of wine in her glass.

"You're welcome, baby. Anything for you." I nodded as I ran my fingers through her hair. I knew I was taking a chance of blowing it, but it just seemed like the right time. The whole night seemed like it was leading up to this.

Damn! My nipples became hard instantly. I'd waited so long for this moment.

Jewel didn't resist, so I kept doing it over and over again. Eventually she tilted her head back, and I kissed her passionately. We stayed out on the balcony kissing and caressing each other. The breeze blowing between us added another layer of sensuality.

I needed to feel Jewel's skin next to mine, so I led her back into the room and gently slipped off her maxi dress. I massaged her feet and rubbed her whole body down. Jewel dozed in and out of sleep, with intermittent moans.

I moved from her feet and began massaging her legs. Then I moved up to her thighs. Jewel let out a gentle sigh when she realized my fingers had moved to her clit. I continued to massage it up and down with my fingers.

"I love your beautiful breasts," I whispered in her ear. I started sucking the nipple of her plump right breast.

By this time Jewel was soaking wet. I continued to massage her clit back and forth. This time, it was with my tongue while I reached up and gently caressed her breasts. I couldn't believe this was finally happening. Even in my best dreams, it was never this good. Jewel was sexier in person than she was in my fantasy.

It didn't take long before she had cum in my mouth and I was savoring the taste of her juices. I wasn't finished giving pleasure to Jewel. I kissed her sensually before I whispered in her ear, "Just lay back, baby. I'm not done with you yet."

I reached into the bedside table and pulled out my strap-on dildo. After adjusting it around my waist, I pulled her legs up and pushed it inside.

"Hmm!" Jewel sighed again.

"Jewel, I love you so much. Please, let me make you mine," I cooed in her ear as my deep thrusts kept coming.

We made love over and over for hours. It was beyond all of my expectations. I was now fully in love with Jewel. I stroked her hair as she slept soundly after our lovemaking. As I stared at her, I knew what I had to do next. In order to keep all of my focus on Jewel, I had to end it with Jamie immediately. Jewel was the most important thing in my life.

Jewel spent the night with me, and the next morning we had a nice breakfast on the balcony. Some eggs, bacon, toast and coffee were our food of choice. I was afraid that the next morning would have been awkward, but it was totally comfortable. Jewel showered while I prepared the breakfast, and then we had a nice conversation about her future. Although I was thinking it, I didn't ask how I was going to fit into her plans.

I got sad when it was time for Jewel to be on her way back to DC. There was a moment when I almost asked her to stay with me, but then I talked myself out of it. I didn't want to come on too fast and strong. I would enjoy the fact that we had one night together and make sure that there were many more.

As soon as Jewel was out the door, I picked up the phone and called Jamie. It wasn't a conversation I was looking forward to having, but it needed to be done, and the sooner the better.

"Hello," Jamie answered.

"Jamie, it's me, Misty."

"Hey, Misty! I'm so happy you called. How are you?"

"I'm good. I was hoping we could talk." I didn't waste any time.

"Of course, baby. I'll always be here to talk whenever you want."

I could already tell Jamie wasn't going to make this easy. *When someone is treating you so nice, how can you just drop him?* I was already feeling guilty, and I hadn't even told Jamie it was over before it even started. I knew I was going to have to stay strong and stick to my guns if I was going to make the break.

"I want to talk about us. I think—"

"I think we make a great pair. Our first go-around was just a trial. I'm ready for this. For you and me."

"Well, you may feel that, but—"

"Hey, Misty, hold on one second. I have another call coming in." Jamie switched over to the other line without even waiting for me to give him permission.

As I listened to the silence on the other end, I started to rehearse what I was about to say when Jamie came back. The only problem was, everything I was rehearsing sounded stupid. After a few attempts to figure out exactly what to say, I gave up. I was going to have to just go with whatever came out and deal with Jamie's reaction.

Once I stopped my rehearsal, I realized I had been on hold for a while, and it started to aggravate me. Why was I holding for so long with someone I was about to dump? I hung up and went to the bedroom to dress for the day.

When I got to the bedroom I noticed that Jewel had left her panties behind. I quickly grabbed them up off the floor and shoved them into my nose. I inhaled her sweet scent, and memories of the previous night flooded my mind. I instantly went right back between Jewel's legs. Just as I was starting to play with my pussy, the phone rang and shocked me out of my memory.

"Hello," I answered in an agitated tone.

"Hey, it's me. Sorry I was on the other line for so long. There's an emergency at work, and I was trying to solve it over the phone. Looks like I have to go in and deal with it. Can we meet up later to discuss us?"

I really didn't want to meet face to face with Jamie. It would be easier for me to end it over the phone, but I just wanted to get back to tending my pussy, so I agreed. I knew, whether over the phone or in person, Jamie wasn't going to take this well.

"Text me the time and place, and I'll be there," I said.

"Will do," Jamie replied, sounding chipper.

"See you later." As I was about to hang up, Jamie had one more thing to say to me.

"Hey, Misty, I'm glad you called." I could tell there was a smile on his face.

Ugh! I thought. *This nigga is trippin'.* I wasn't looking forward to meeting him later.

I hung up the phone and picked up right where I had left off. My hand went directly to my clit as I lay back on the bed and closed my eyes. In an instant I was picturing Jewel between my legs, and all thoughts of Jamie had disappeared.

Chapter 21

Jewel

"Wicked Realization"

My pussy was aching, along with me feeling sick. Laying on my side didn't help either. A wave of nausea took over. I ran to the bathroom, barely making it to the stool. I vomited so hard, it even came out of my nose. Afterward, I looked in the mirror and realized that I was naked. I cleaned myself up and slowly walked out of the bathroom, afraid of what or who I may see next. There, lying in the bed was Misty, and she was naked as well.

Oh ,shit! What have I done? I thought to myself. I wracked my brain trying to figure it out.

Bits and pieces of the night before started to come back to me. One of the empty wine bottles was scattered on the carpet. I started to feel nervous and jittery. My hands were shaking, and my brain was racing. *I just had sex with not only a woman, but a woman who happens to be in love with me. After Sasha I vowed I would never do this again. We can't just be friends now. Misty will want more. This all happened so fast. Did Misty take advantage of me?*

I didn't know what to think. I started getting afraid that Misty was still working with the feds, so I didn't want to do anything to piss her off. Instead of running out of there, I stayed around and acted cool. Luckily for me, Misty didn't move when I jumped out of bed to throw up, so I just slipped right back next to her. This time I nudged her a little bit so she would wake up.

"Hey, Jewel," Misty said as she wiped her eyes and stretched.

I smiled. "Hey, yourself."

"Stay for breakfast?" Misty asked. It sounded like a question, but I wasn't sure if she was telling me to stay. I decided it better to stay and try and make her happy. Hopefully this little fling would just fade away. I didn't need no cop pissed off at me.

"Yeah. Let me shower first."

"You shower, I'll cook." Misty put her robe on while I went to the bathroom.

I tried acting as normal as possible throughout breakfast. Misty kept asking me about my future and what I was planning. Not wanting to give up too much, I made up some bullshit about taking night courses. I was pretty vague about the whole thing though.

After breakfast Misty tried to get me to stay longer, but I put a stop to that. Told her I needed to get back to Shakira and take care of her daughter.

I breathed a huge sigh of relief when I reached my car. On my way home, Misty began blowing up my cell phone. She called so many times that I shut off my phone. Driving like a bat out of hell, I rushed home.

"Hey, Auntie Jewel, I made you a picture," Kelly said as soon as I walked in the door.

"Thanks, baby." I smiled and gave her a hug.

Shakira could see how upset I was and told her little one to go in her room and color. "Jewel, what's going on?" she asked as soon as the coast was clear.

"I can't tell you. I'm too embarrassed," I replied, crying and hiding my face.

"Listen, there's nothing you can tell me that I haven't already heard. Girl, I'm all ears."

"Last night I went to see Misty. You know the woman that was in the restaurant staring us down? That's her. She was following me."

"Yeah. So you knew her? What she following you for?"

"She's a friend from the past. I don't want to go into all the details, but she was a close friend of mine, until I found out she worked for the police. Anyway, I was vulnerable because I just left Touch. I just went over there to talk, and this morning I woke up in her bed. I didn't mean for this to happen. She is in love with me. I'm not ready for this, let alone with a woman. You know what I went through with Sasha. She even ruined our friendship. So after her, I vowed I would never go there again."

"I understand. You know I know more than anyone what's it like to be vulnerable. Why don't you take a long hot bath and get some rest? I'll make you my home remedy soup. It can sober anyone up. Then we can figure out what you need to do. My first thought is for you to just tell Misty the truth—You ain't feeling her or any woman, especially right now when you are trying to get your life back."

"How did you know I was drinking?" I said, full of shame.

Shakira giggled. "It's on your breath and comin' out your skin."

I playfully smacked Shakira on her shoulder and went to the bathroom for a good soak. While in the hot bath, I began thinking about what Shakira had said. The thing was, I was kind of feeling Misty. She was seeming really genuine and kind to me. I couldn't believe she was still working for the police, with the way she was acting. All of her advice had been to get away from Touch. If she was still looking to get him, she would've wanted me close, so I could feed her information. I just wasn't sure if I was ready to be with a woman full time. Being a lesbian had never seemed like a lifestyle I would live.

As I thought more and more about Misty, I kept thinking, *I could really like this girl.* Which scared me and confused me. The only decision I could come up with was to take it slow and not jump into anything too fast. I was going to make sure to stick to my new motto—It's all about me and what makes me happy.

With that thought, I closed my eyes and enjoyed the warm bath. I would deal with Misty later.

Chapter 22

Misty

"It's Over"

As soon as I finished masturbating, I called Jewel. I needed to speak to her about Jamie. She was so strong the way she dealt with Touch that I wanted her to help me through my ordeal. I wanted her to counsel me on how she got her strength, to give me the confidence she had. When Jewel didn't answer, I figured she either didn't hear the phone or wasn't able to get to it in time. I called right back, and the outcome was the same. I continued to call back to back with the same result. The last time I called, instead of ringing, it went straight to voice mail. I didn't want to believe that she had ignored my calls, so I told myself that she must be in a poor signal area.

I got concerned that perhaps something was wrong with Jewel. I turned on the local news station to see if there were any reports of accidents. After sitting in front of the television for an hour listening to the same stories over and over, I turned it off. I was satisfied that Jewel had not been harmed. So then why didn't she answer? We had such a great night together, and the morning was so special. It couldn't be that she was avoiding me.

I didn't have much time to stress over Jewel's actions as Jamie texted me the address of where we were meeting. I was so consumed with thoughts of Jewel that I had completely forgotten about Jamie and our meeting. I took my time getting ready to go out, stalling for as long as I could. This was the last thing I wanted to do, but I wasn't going to back down. I always faced my problems head on and tackled them, and I wasn't about to change. I slung my purse over my shoulder and headed out the door, hoping it would go easy.

Jamie was already waiting at the restaurant when I arrived, which didn't surprise me, since I was a half an hour late. That was done on purpose to try and piss Jamie off. My new plan was to try and get him to want to break it off with me. I figured the bitchier I was, the less likely he would want to be with me.

"Hey, sorry I'm late. I took a nap and slept a little late," I said as I approached.

"No problem. I'm just happy you got here. You must have really needed the extra sleep." He smiled and went in for a hug.

I kept my hands at my side and didn't reciprocate his affection. *Damn, that didn't work!* He was acting like it was fine to be kept waiting. This wasn't going to be easy.

The hostess sat us at a small booth with a nice view out the window. If I had been there with Jewel, I would have thought it to be a romantic spot, but since I was with Jamie, it was just another place to sit and eat. I saw Jamie slip the hostess some cash and give her a look. He must have requested a romantic table when he arrived and rewarded the hostess for a job well done. Jamie was pulling out all the stops to try and woo me. I was going to have to counter his politeness with some downright dirty-ass bitch.

"This place doesn't look very expensive," I said as I sat down.

"Does it matter?"

"It just kind of shows how you think of me. Taking me to a mediocre place." I frowned as I looked around the room.

"Let's go somewhere else," he said, staying upbeat. "Wherever you want."

"No. I don't feel like driving all over town. Let's just get this over with."

Jamie either didn't hear what I said or chose to ignore it. He just shrugged his shoulders and said, "Okay, whatever you want."

Seriously this was not the way I thought he would be reacting. I mean, I was acting disinterested and bored the second I met him, and he seemed immune to it. Damn, he was going to make me work for this breakup.

"It smells funny in here. Are you wearing cologne?" I scrunched my nose and sniffed the air near Jamie.

"I'm wearing my usual CK One."

"Can cologne go rotten?"

"I don't know." He shrugged his shoulders again.

Not even a direct insult was doing anything to upset him. Inside I was going crazy. I wanted this to be quick and easy and make Jamie feel like he was the one doing the breaking up. Nothing was working, but I was going to hold steady with my plan though.

I looked at the menu and decided on a chicken salad. You know I needed to look fit for Jewel, so my diet had started. After deciding, I just sat there and stared out the window, looking as bored as I possibly could. I even sighed a few times to draw Jamie's attention away from his menu.

Jamie placed the menu on the table in front of him and folded his hands together. "So did you see anything you like?" he asked.

"Yes." I continued looking out the window.

"Good. I'm going to have their burger and fries."

"Keep eating like that, you'll get fat."

He chuckled. "I suppose you're right."

I was now furious inside. He wasn't getting offended by anything I was saying. *What is up with this guy? Was he that in love with me that it didn't matter what I said? I might need to rethink this situation. Maybe I should stay with this guy if he was going to let me act how I wanted. He could fund my life, and I could have Jewel on the side.*

The waitress came over and took our order, and I went directly back to looking out the window. I was now thinking about living my life with Jamie and having Jewel on the side. Could I make that work? As I was fantasizing about that life, Jamie interrupted.

"You said earlier that you wanted to talk about us."

"Yeah. Until you so rudely kept me waiting on hold." I couldn't help being rude now. I had come in with that mindset, and now I couldn't drop it. Damn. I wanted to feel Jamie out and see if he would be up for my arrangement.

"I'm sorry about that."

I took a sip of my Diet Coke and proceeded. "About us. I was thinking that we could date but see other people as well."

Jamie looked perplexed. I couldn't tell what his reaction was by the look on his face. He seemed to be thinking it over. He just kept looking at me and not saying anything, which was starting to freak me out.

"So? What do you think?" I asked.

Now it was Jamie's turn to stare out the window. What was this dude's problem? It was a simple question. This non-answer shit was annoying me.

"So?" I asked again.

Jamie snapped at me. "I'm thinking."

"Chill, muthafucka. Don't snap at me."

"I'm sorry," he said.

The waitress came back over with our food and was about to say something, but she noticed the energy at our table and decided to keep her mouth shut and walk away.

As soon as she was out of range I resumed. "Whatever. Just answer me. Yes or no?"

"Is there someone else? Is that why?"

"No."

"Then why would you ask that?"

"Let's just say, I'm keeping my options open."

"Why can't it just be us and no one else? I want you to move in with me. If we both work, we can save up, buy a big house, and have kids."

Jamie reached for my hand, but I snatched it away. His little pussy-whipped act was starting to wear thin.

"Are you trippin'? I have my own place, and I'm damn sure not about to move in with you or start saving money with you."

"But the other night together was so special."

"Oh, shit. You have got to be kidding me. If I wanted to live with a bitch I would."

Those words made me realize that I was crazy to think I could make anything with Jamie work. My heart and soul were all for Jewel.

"In fact, I want to live with a woman. We have fucked, and I am in love with her, not you. You may be acting like a female right now, but you will never replace the real thing. There is room for one woman in my life. Later, bitch. Don't try contacting me ever again."

Before I even had a chance to stand, Jamie shot up from his chair and screamed, "Fuck you," at the top of his lungs, threw his plate of food through the window, and stormed out of the restaurant.

Everyone turned to stare at me sitting at the table alone and in shock. The whole restaurant was completely silent, stunned at what they just witnessed. I sheepishly looked around the dining room at all the customers. I was embarrassed, to say the least.

I tried to stand up and act like I wasn't fazed, but I'm sure I looked rattled. I was planning on walking out with my head held high and a little dignity, but that was stopped immediately. The restaurant manager came over with two waiters and blocked me from leaving.

"Ma'am, I'm afraid you can't leave. Your guest just vandalized our restaurant."

I was snapped back to reality. Cops were going to get involved in this. It would probably be department gossip in a matter of minutes. I had to make sure I wasn't turned into a department joke.

"Yes, I understand. I'm sorry. I was just so stunned, I don't know what I was thinking. Let me pay for the damage and the meal." I pulled out a credit card.

"It won't be that easy. There will be insurance involved, and I'm not even sure how much it is going to cost to fix. We'll need to call the police. I'm sorry."

"No, don't. Please. Let's work it out on our own and not involve anyone else."

The manager thought about it for a minute and decided to not call the police. You know I was relieved. We went back to his office and got down to business. We decided that I wouldn't leave until it was all worked out. He called his contractor and explained the situation.

After several hours and several different quotes to fix the window, we came to an agreement. I gave the manager my credit card number to use after the work was finished. I assured him that I would be monitoring my credit statements, and if there was one odd charge, or I was charged one more dollar than the quoted price, there would be hell to pay.

As I was leaving, I spotted the waitress who had helped me earlier. Luckily she was working a double shift. I walked over to her and handed her a fifty-dollar bill.

"I apologize about earlier," I said and walked out embarrassed but free. It was the most expensive breakup of my life.

Chapter 23

Lisa

"Target on Your Back"

I looked down at my ringing cell phone. This was the third time that my girlfriend Sylvia had called me. Everyone knew not to disturb me when I was tuning into my reality shows, so I wasn't about to answer. This night I was watching *Basketball Wives*. Those were my girls.

I couldn't take the constant texts and phone calls one after the other, so I answered. Luckily, the show went to a commercial. "Hello?" I answered, annoyed.

"Did you get my texts?" she asked.

"No," I replied.

"I figured that much. Because if you did get my texts, you would have been here by now."

Now Sylvia had my full attention. I pressed pause on the DVR, so I wouldn't miss a second of my show. "Been where?"

"Okay, listen to me very closely. Touch is at the club, Tigerland, with some girl. I thought I should let you know. I would have busted him in the head with a bottle myself, but I'm on a date."

"That's okay. Let me do my own dirty work. So is that chick better-looking than me? Is she light-skinned or dark? Is she ghetto or proper? I need details." I wanted to know what I was up against.

"Don't worry. She's no competition. I've got to go. I've been in the bathroom too long blowing you up. I don't want Jarrod to think I ditched him," Sylvia said before hanging up the phone.

Sylvia was a loyal friend, so it was no surprise to me that she'd made this call. She knew how bad I wanted to fuck with Touch. She even tried to tag along and help, but this was my deal and my deal only.

This was one time I had to put *Basketball Wives* aside. I hurried to put on a cute top, jeans, and stiletto heels. I was going to be the shining star of the night, so I needed to dress the part. I grabbed my co-star, my gun, and put it in my purse. If things went as planned, my gun would end up inside Touch's mouth. I was about to take this game to a whole new level. My mouth started to water, thinking about him pleading for his life.

I was happy that Sylvia had called me. We had just talked about how I was aggravated because the past few days, Touch's house was deserted, and that chick, Jewel, was nowhere to be found. I knew doing something to her would have definitely caught Touch's attention and possibly pushed him over the edge.

Every time I thought about how he spat on me and beat on me, I got angrier and angrier. Repressed rage and aggression was taking a toll on me. My hair was thinning out, and most days, I felt jittery. Getting revenge had become crack to me, and I was an addict. I wasn't sure what my end game was with Touch, but I just knew how much satisfaction I got out of harassing his ass.

After getting dressed, I hopped in my car and rushed to the club. Since I arrived so late, the club parking lot was half-empty. Knowing Touch very well, I knew he would be the last to come out of the building. That nigga loved his drink and would always close bars down.

An hour passed, and cars continued to leave the lot one by one. I watched the club door, patiently waiting for Touch. The waiting was making me tired, and I started to doze off when he finally came out with this mysterious girl. They stumbled across the parking lot to Touch's truck. He had her pressed up against the truck while he felt on her ass and managed to feel up her dress. With the way they were going at it, I thought they would have fucked right in the parking lot if so many people weren't around. It made me disgusted to watch them go at it like they were. I had reached my boiling point.

I quietly but quickly got out of my car, took my gun out of my purse, and fired one shot in the air. Instant chaos erupted in the parking lot. People started scattering and ducking to the ground. Women were screaming, and their boyfriends were trying to hush them up.

My second shot was aimed at Touch, but I missed and hit his car window. My third shot, I had a good aim at him. He was splayed out on the ground in plain view. My eyes got as big as saucers. He was going to die this night, and I would finally be able to move on with my life.

I calmly aimed the gun right at his head and started taking steps closer to make sure I hit his ass. Right as I was about to pull the trigger, something hit me like a ton of rocks, knocking the gun from my hands and forcing me to hit the ground.

I scrambled to turn around to see a two-hundred-pound police offer coming at me like a raging bull. Before I knew it, he was on top of me.

"Officer, that man has been trying to kill me," I screamed, spitting bits of dirt out of my mouth.

"Lady, you're the one with the gun!"

"It's for protection."

"Man, y'all just don't know what this girl has put me through. Justice is finally going to be served. I ain't never been a fan of the police, but I'm sure glad you're here tonight!" Touch said, after running over to me.

The cops flipped me on my stomach and handcuffed me. Touch was taunting my ass the entire time. Like he was the one responsible for me getting arrested. That shit pissed me off too.

When the cops helped me to stand up, I tried to go right at Touch. I was kicking like a donkey, just trying to inflict any sort of pain I could on him. I hit him in the leg, but all he did was laugh.

"See, officers? You see what she is like? This bitch is crazy," Touch said, pointing at me.

Meanwhile, the bitch that Touch was messing with before I interrupted them was crying hysterically on the arm of some other dude. I guess that guy saw an opportunity to swoop in, and he took it. Served Touch right to lose that bitch. I got some satisfaction out of seeing that.

The cops put me in the back of the car and slammed the door after me. I started kicking the cage that separated the front from the back. Then I tried to kick out the windows, and when that didn't work, I went back to the cage. All the while, the cops were talking to Touch, no doubt getting his version of the events between us. Which was fine with me, because when we saw each other in court, it would be my word against his. If I was a betting woman, I would put money on me to convince the jury that I was innocent.

The crowd around the parking lot had dispersed by the time the police were done talking to Touch. His little hussy left with the other dude, which made me so happy. I had tired myself out with all the kicking I had done. My right foot was killing me. I was kicking so hard, I had actually broken a bone in it. I would make Touch pay for that when I saw him again. I figured if he caused me to break a bone in my body, he needed to have a broken bone in his body as well. *Which bone would it be?* I thought. *I think I'll break his back. Lay his ass up in bed for a few months. That'll teach him.* I smiled as the cops got into the car.

Touch came up to the car window before they pulled off and said, "You getting what you deserve, bitch. You going to jail, psycho." Then he started laughing at me.

"You stupid muthafucka. I got my revenge on you, when I snuck in your house and beat the shit out of you. I had you scared for days." I laughed as the car pulled away.

Chapter 24

Touch

"Family Ties"

After that incident with Lisa, I made a vow to be extra careful about where I stick my dick. Lisa had me shook. The whole time I was thinking one of Jewel's stragglers had beat the hell out of me that night. Come to find out, it was Lisa all along. I couldn't believe I let a bitch do that to me. I felt like a damn fool. I was definitely going to make sure no one on the street found out about that shit.

When I sat and thought about things, I realized Lisa had been stalking Jewel and me for the entire time since I was dismissed from the assault charges on her. She was bitter, angry, and wanted nothing more than to see me die. I should have known it was her. I had a hunch, but I couldn't convince myself that a bitch would be that crazy or clever.

After that incident I couldn't sleep, tossing and turning in my hotel room all night. The room was nice enough, but I didn't feel like wasting all my money on some bullshit uptight hotel. I wanted to use it to buy me a nice house. The bed in the hotel was a far cry from my king-sized bed I was used to at home.

After tossing and turning all night, I finally looked at the clock, and it was eight a.m. I was cranky as hell from a long night and a lack of sleep. I wanted to stay in bed all day and try to get some shut-eye, but my boy Jimmy was getting out of jail today. That was motivation enough for me to get out of bed and get dressed.

I was happy Jimmy was getting released because I felt like there was so much he could teach me about the game. There was only so much he could teach me from the inside. I knew my street IQ was about to get a bump up. I had visions of even more money coming my way and one day running my own international drug ring.

After a quick breakfast, I picked up Deuce, and we headed over to Jimmy's girl's place, so we could straighten out this missing money. On the ride over, Deuce was in a talkative mood, which was surprising. Normally he was a man of few words. When he did open his mouth, it was only about one thing and one thing only—the year of 1973 when he ruled the streets, and now he walks those same streets.

I was sick and tired of his same old stories. It was like he stopped living after 1973. At first, I liked hearing the stories, but after hearing them over and over, I wanted to punch him in his mouth. I wanted to scream, "Shut the fuck up, you old fool!" but I would just tune out instead, and continue doing whatever it was I was doing at the time.

This day he was talking about how happy he was Jimmy was getting out but that he wasn't sure if Jimmy would be able to survive on the streets anymore. He kept talking about the missing money and asking me if I knew anything about it.

"If you took it, you can tell me," he said. "I won't tell Jimmy. You'll just have to split it with me."

"The fuck kinda snake you think I am? I didn't steal shit. My money was always tight."

After that, we pretty much rode in silence. Occasionally Deuce would say some stupid shit like, "I can't wait to see Jimmy."

Deuce started in with his trip down memory lane, but we had gotten to the house before he could really get deep into his 1973 stories. I couldn't get out of the car fast enough.

When we walked in the house, Jimmy was sitting on the couch, sipping a glass of Rémy. This old dude was slick. When he saw us, he put the drink down as he stood to greet us.

"'S up, Jimmy! You home, big man," I said after we walked into the living room of his house.

I started to give him a hug, but he stopped me with a handshake. I guess he didn't like to be touched or some shit. He shook Deuce's hand as well. He was acting real cold toward us. I was expecting a warmer return from him. He was mad cool in the joint, so I just expected even more of it now that he was on the outside. Especially since I had been making so much money for old dude.

Before I knew it, a gun was at the side of Deuce's head. When I moved back to get out of the way, the gun was pointed at me. I had no idea what the reason for this show of aggression was. Had Jimmy been playing me this whole time? He set my ass up. He softened me up in the joint, got me connected on the outside, so I could make him money. Then when he got out and everything was in place, he would off me and take all the profits for himself.

"Yo', man, Jimmy—" I said with my hands in the air, wondering what the hell was going on.

"My money is missing, and one of you have it. I need answers," he demanded, cutting me off.

"Jim, it's me, man. I took it. Please, man, just put the gun down."

I looked over to see Deuce on his knees, begging for his life, a big wet spot in front of his pants. I shook my head. This nigga was a fucking disgrace. All the talk about how bad-ass he was back in the day, and he punks out like this? At least he could have tried lying for a while, tried blaming it on me, something to save his ass, but to just cop to it so fast, that shit was embarrassing.

"I was shaving ten grand off the money here and there. I have about fifty thousand dollars in the safe. It's all yours. Take it, man. Just don't kill me, Jim. I know it was wrong, and I felt bad about doing it. That's why I told you. I was going to give it back. I promise. You gotta believe me."

Deuce continued to beg like a little bitch, piss running down his leg. I swear I started to smell shit too. Absolutely disgraceful. I couldn't stand watching his ass beg like a woman.

"Man, have some fuckin' pride!" I yelled, annoyed not only by Deuce robbing Jimmy but by his bitch-ass attitude. "You fucked up. Now be a man about it."

"How could you do it, Deuce? We've been friends over thirty years, man," Jimmy said, shaking his head, still with gun in hand.

I looked at Jimmy, and he had a sadness in his eyes. I could tell it hurt him that his good friend had betrayed him.

"You fucked up our bond when you let Touch in. You have never taken to no dude like Touch before, so it was mind-boggling for me. Jealousy kicked in, and I was planning to pin the missing money on Touch. I know I was wrong. Come on, man. Please. Have sympathy on an old friend."

Only mere seconds passed before Jimmy shot Deuce twice in the head like it was nothing. Good thing he did because if Deuce had walked out that spot alive, I'd have killed him myself for trying to set me up.

We silently stood there watching the blood ooze from Deuce's skull. His eyes were still open, and I felt like he was staring at me. I thought, *Good riddance, you thieving bastard!*

Jimmy's face was tight. He looked pained at the sight of his long-time friend lying dead in front of him.

"Come on, let's take care of this," Jimmy said, signaling in the direction of Deuce's dead body.

I took his shoulders, and Jimmy took his feet, and we moved Deuce's body into the bathtub. Jimmy left the bathroom and returned with two saws and a couple of butcher knives. We began the process of chopping Deuce's body into pieces. We wrapped the parts up in garbage bags and placed them into storage bins. We threw them into the trunk, and Jimmy and I drove to the Chesapeake Bay Bridge in silence. I knew this must have been hard for Jimmy, but we both knew the business, so there was no need to talk about it.

Seeing things like this made me never want to get close to nobody. I would hate to have to kill my best friend over some shit like this. In my opinion, there is no room for friendship in this game. I would learn everything I could from Jimmy, but I wasn't going to get too attached to liking this dude. If the day ever came where I had to take him out, I didn't want it to be hard on me mentally or emotionally.

We stopped at the bridge and emptied the trunk, being careful that no one saw what we were doing. It seemed like each splash echoed for miles, it was so quiet.

"That was hard," Jimmy said when all the bins had been dumped.

I didn't say anything. I just shook my head. I didn't know if he meant killing his best friend and chopping him up or throwing those heavy-ass bins into the water.

For the next few weeks, Jimmy and I worked the streets ourselves, never once mentioning what had happened. It was an understanding that we had. It seemed to take Jimmy a few days to get out of the funk he was in after killing Deuce.

Soon, it came out that Deuce wasn't paying people their agreed-upon cuts. People on the street were pissed. Deuce would short them and just keep stalling when they came to get the rest of their money. Word of mouth about Jimmy's operation was not good. He was blacklisted; no one wanted anything to do with his business. Jimmy's empire was fucked up, but I knew he had every intention of putting it back together, and I planned on being by his side the entire way.

"Deuce was right about me taking to you so well," Jimmy commented one day while we were on the road collecting money.

"Feeling's mutual, man," I told him. "From day one I looked up to you. You always gonna be cool with me. You picked me up in a big way when I was down."

"It's more to it than that. I'm just gon' be straight-forward with you, man." Jimmy paused for a minute and looked out the window at the passing buildings. He continued to look away from me. "Touch, I'm your grandfather. I'm your father's father."

"What?" I said, shocked and in disbelief. I almost ran off the fucking road. "My mother told me my father had passed. I never knew the man."

"Boy, I know. He is alive and well in Connecticut." I couldn't believe my ears. I had mixed emotions inside. How could I have gone so long thinking my dad was dead and this entire time he was living in another state? Why did my moms lie to me? I couldn't under-stand why she would do that. Why didn't Jimmy come to me sooner and tell me who he was? I wanted to hug him and punch him all at the same time. My mind was going in a million directions. I wanted to cry, I wanted to scream, I wanted to fight. I was crazy confused.

I slammed on the brakes and made a U-turn.

"Where you going, boy?" Jimmy asked.

"I've gotta talk to my moms about this shit, man. I'm all fucked up in the head right now."

We went back and forth for a second about whether that was a good idea, but in the end Jimmy agreed to come with me to my mom's house. I had to know the truth. Growing up without a father because my mother purposely wanted it that way was fucked up.

I raced over to my mom's house, not caring that I was breaking the speed limit and in danger of getting pulled over by the cops.

Jimmy and I walked into my mother's living room. I called out to her. "Mom!"

"Touch, is that you? I cooked some lunch. Do you want"—The bowl of grits in her hands fell to the carpet when she saw Jimmy's face.

"Why? Why would you lie to me about my father?" I asked with tears in my eyes.

"I knew this day would come but not so soon." My mom turned toward Jimmy. She looked defeated. "What did you tell him, Jim?"

"Not much. I'll leave the explaining up to you."

"Trayvon, sit down, baby." My mom pointed to a bar stool that sat at the breakfast bar to the kitchen. "Your uncles, my brothers, used to work for Jimmy back in the day. That's how I met your father. We both were very young when I got pregnant, and I knew my mother would never approve of the baby or him. Momma forced me to live with my aunt in Alabama 'til I gave birth to you, and then I could move back. She was ashamed and didn't want her beloved church members to know I had gotten pregnant out of wedlock. When I returned I learned that your father and my cousin were in a relationship. That tore me apart, Trayvon. You don't understand. I loved that man. When he cheated on me, it killed me. I couldn't bear the pain. From that day forth, I vowed I would never speak to him again."

I felt her pain and definitely understood where she was coming from, but I still didn't agree with her decision. I felt like she had deprived me of a relationship with my father my entire life. So many nights I would lie in my bed and wish I had a dad to talk to, to ask for advice. I may never have gotten into the drug game if he had been around. I should have been allowed to make my own decisions about my father.

"Mom, you should have told me. You just can't make decisions on my life like that," I screamed at her and walked out. I needed time to process everything that was just said to me. I didn't know how to handle all of the emotions I was feeling, so I just jetted.

I dropped Jimmy off back at his house. On the way back to his place, I didn't say a word to him. I was angry with him and didn't want to hear his bullshit at the moment. I told him that I needed a few days off to clear my head. He agreed that it was a good idea. We said a sorrowful good-bye, and I drove back to the hotel, my head pounding from all the emotions and stress I was feeling.

I stopped at the front desk, and they gave me some Advil for my headache. But what I needed right at the time more than anything was to talk to Jewel. She was the only one that could comfort me. She knew how much I had longed for a father in my life. She would be able to understand my pain and anguish. I called the realtor and pretended I was interested in buying the house but would only speak to Jewel. It took a little convincing, but she finally gave me the number.

"Hey," I said as soon as she answered.

"Hey," she said back in a flat tone.

"You busy?" I asked her.

"Not really. Right now I'm free, but I have a doctor's appointment later on today."

"Is everything okay?" I asked, truly concerned that something was wrong with the baby.

"Everything is fine. I'm just going for a checkup."

"Okay, cool. Well, can you meet at Mahi Mah's by the oceanfront? I really need to talk to you."

"Okay, I will meet you. But don't try no stupid shit because I won't hesitate to shoot your ass."

Chapter 25

Jewel

"'Til Death Do Us Part"

"Are you sure you don't need me to go with you?" Misty asked, while giving me a hug. "I don't mind."

I had come back to Virginia to go to the doctors and take care of a few things, and Misty was nice enough to let me sleep at her place. Well, I'm sure the fact that we were having sex every night didn't hurt. Anyway, lucky for Touch, I was in town because if I was in DC, I would never have agreed to meet up with him.

"I'll be fine," I said with a fake smile.

The truth was, I felt sick to my stomach and vomited again the previous night. At the time, Misty was asleep and didn't hear me. If she knew I didn't feel well, she would have insisted on coming along with me. It was strange, but it felt nice sleeping next to Misty. Plus, she was pampering me constantly. No man had done that to me for a while.

"Just in case I'm not home, here is your own house key," she said, handing it to me.

"Thank you." I nodded.

"Have a great day. Hopefully, you won't run into traffic," Misty yelled, as I headed out the door.

I rushed to the oceanfront to meet Touch. I prayed everything would go well, and I could eat and get out in time to make my doctor's appointment. When I walked in the restaurant, I saw Touch right away. The hostess met me at the door. After she sat me down at the table where Touch was sitting, I looked into his eyes. Surprisingly enough, I felt nothing for him at all. I guess, once my mind was made up, my heart had no choice but to follow the same path as well. It's funny, because the way I used to feel when I looked into Touch's eyes was the way I felt when I looked into Misty's eyes.

While we ate lunch Touch revealed the story about his mother lying about his father being dead. The whole story was just so sad. Maybe if Touch's father had been in his life, he wouldn't have turned out the way he did. Listening to the story though, I kept thinking, *Like father, like son.* Touch's dad was a cheat, and so was his son. Still, I felt sympathy for Touch. All the years we were together, he always wished he could see his father. I felt his mother was very selfish and only thinking about herself.

"Listen, Jewel, I need you to come back home. I love you, and I miss you. I'm sorry for everything I put you through. Hearing this story about my father makes me want to be a great father to our baby and a better man for you," Touch pleaded, touching my hand.

"Touch, I can't do that," I stated, shaking my head and removing my hand from his.

"Why? We have been together too long to just end it."

"Yeah, that's what I used to think. Touch, you have hurt me so bad. As bad as your father hurt your mother, maybe even worse. At least he never laid his hands on her like you did to me. I'm tired, and I have reached my limit. Besides, the house is going to be sold next week. In fact, I'm meeting with the realtor at the house today at six to finalize a few things. I've moved on with my life, Touch. I moved out of Virginia over a month ago."

"Why would you do that without talking to me first? I understand if you don't want to be with me, but what about our baby? How can I be a father to my child if you're in an entirely different state? It will be like my father and me."

"Enough of the baby talk," I spat, frustrated. It was time he knew the truth. "There is no damn baby, Touch."

"What?"

"You heard me, Touch. I had an abortion, okay. You were on the run, and we were having major problems in our relationship. I didn't know how or when I would see you, and I barely had enough money to take care of myself, much less a baby. There was no way I could bring a child into a situation like that. There was no way I would want my child to have an unstable father like you."

"Bitch!" He reached for my throat.

I quickly jumped up and threw my water in his face. "Don't make me pull out on you," I said, going into my purse to grab my gun.

Touch called me every name in the book using every profanity you can think of. He pushed the table over, and people all over the restaurant began to stare at us.

I pulled my gun out and pointed it at Touch. Everyone in the restaurant scattered. We had a little standoff, neither of us saying anything, just staring into each other's eyes.

Finally, Touch left with tears in his eyes, but I refused to shed a tear for that fucker. I calmly put my gun away, paid the bill for the little that we ate, and left the restaurant.

On the way to the doctor's office, I started thinking about everything that just happened, and I actually started to feel a little guilty for what I did. I realized by the tears in Touch's eyes that he really wanted a son. Touch had twin girls that he loved dearly, but because of a domestic dispute between him and his baby mother, he hadn't seen them in months. My baby was probably his only hope of filling that void. Now with the news of his father and everything else, he was fragile. I began to get a little choked up as I pulled up to the doctor's office, but again I refused to drop a tear.

I probably should have told him sooner that I'd had an abortion, but I was afraid that he would've put a beating on me when I told him. I didn't know what I would do when the time came for me to have the baby, but I knew I was going to avoid telling him for as long as I could. *Oh well, Touch brought this all on himself.*

The waiting room was empty when I arrived. "Hello. I'm here for my appointment," I announced as I walked to the receptionist's desk to sign in.

"Hi, Jewel. Fill out these forms. Here is a pen. After that, I will need a urine sample from you for a routine check. The urine cups are in the bathroom with your patient information already labeled on it," the receptionist said to me.

I loved this doctor's office. They had everything all ready for me. All I had to do was show up, and they took care of it all. So much better than the ghetto clinics I used to go through. Those places were third world.

"Thank you," I replied, nodding.

On the form, I decided to put Misty's address as my current address. To be honest, I was feeling Misty and had decided to tell her I wanted to move in when I got home later. It just felt right to me. She treated me the way no man had ever treated me. We'd started out as friends, and it was so easy to talk with her. It just seemed natural to me that we would be lovers. Every time I thought of her, I would smile.

With the form filled out and my mood feeling good, I went to the restroom and tried my best to pee, but I couldn't get even a tinkle. I went back to the waiting room for a while to wait it out.

Ten minutes later I went back into the bathroom, but I still couldn't pee. I didn't know what was going on with me. I was getting sick a lot, and now I couldn't pee. I was getting a little concerned that there might be something seriously wrong with me.

"Excuse me," I said to the nurse behind the counter. "Do you have any water?"

"Honey, are you having trouble giving us a urine sample?" she inquired.

"Yes, I am." I laughed, a bit embarrassed.

"There's a water fountain down the hall. Drink till your heart is content. Wait fifteen minutes, and I'm sure nature will come calling."

"Thank you," I said and headed to the water fountain.

I guzzled four cups of water, and fifteen minutes later I certainly had to pee. The nurse's plan worked. I peed about three times waiting for the doctor to come in. My legs felt cold as I sat there in the gown they had provided for me.

I thought of Misty and started daydreaming about our future together. I hadn't been this happy in a long time. Touch had put me through so much, I had forgotten what happy really felt like.

I was brought back to reality from a knock on the door. I still had a huge smile on my face from my daydream when my doctor entered. "Come in," I said.

"Jewel, sorry for the delay. I had a false alarm with another patient. How have you been?" Dr. Gills started looking over my chart.

"Okay. And you?"

"My kids are growing and eating everything in sight. My husband just bought another motorbike. Life is crazy." Dr. Gills stopped talking as she read my chart. "Well, well, well, looking at your lab work, it looks like you may not be far behind me because you're pregnant. Welcome to the crazy life of husband and kids," Dr. Gills said with a huge grin.

"What?"

We instinctively hugged each other.

"Jewel, I didn't stutter. You're pregnant, honey. And based on your last period, you're about six weeks."

"Wow! Unbelievable!" I said, letting out a loud sigh. I was in a little bit of shock.

"Jewel, you have options, which we can discuss. Now I need to examine you. So if you can just lie back."

My brain was racing during the entire exam. How did this happen? I can't believe I just told Touch there was no baby and there actually was. Now it made sense why I was getting sick so much lately. I can't wait to tell Misty. What will Misty think? Does she even want kids? Even though I didn't know how Misty felt about children, I wasn't afraid to tell her, like I was with Touch. I wasn't afraid of catching a beating from Misty. That was for sure.

After she finished, I requested the nurse perform a blood test to ensure the test results were accurate. Sure enough, the blood test confirmed what Dr. Gills had already told me. Now the reality really set in. I was going to be a mother.

Dr. Gills and I discussed all of my options. I could abort it, but I wasn't going through that again. I could put it up for adoption, but I didn't want my baby growing up in foster homes or going to a bad family. The only option I considered was having the baby and being the best damn mother I could be.

I was so happy when I left the doctor's office. Driving home, I did some calculating, and if my calculations were right, Touch had gotten me pregnant as soon as he came home from jail. I panicked thinking about him. I didn't know what to do. Should I tell him or keep it a secret?

I desperately needed to talk to Misty. Anytime I found myself in a bind or didn't know what to do, she was always my savior. She had the answer to everything.

I rushed back to the house to talk to her. As I walked in, I heard my name, but it wasn't being said to greet me. It was said like someone was talking about me. I paused at the front door. I heard Misty say on the phone, "Jewel has already agreed to testify, so that's a wrap."

I stood at the door and continued to listen.

"The case is solid this time," Misty said. "Captain, no room for fuckup. In fact, I know where Touch is. We can do the sting tomorrow. I can't wait to officially be back on the force."

It felt like my stomach had dropped out my asshole. My head began to spin. My world collapsed in an instant. One minute my future was so bright and happy, the next, it gets crushed by the woman who I thought I loved. I had been used once again by Misty.

I grasped my heart and quickly walked out the house. I was struggling for air when I got in the car. I felt like I was having a fucking panic attack. I couldn't believe that bitch was using me to get rank back on her job. Tears began to run down my face as I started the car and pulled off. I didn't know what to think or who to trust. I couldn't believe I'd let this happen again. *Did she even love me? People are always betraying me*, I thought as I drove to the house to meet the real estate agent.

I tried to call Touch, but he didn't answer. I sent him a text asking him to meet me at the house. I wanted to come clean to him about everything, including Misty. He was the only person I felt I could turn to. My only hope was that he would take me back and keep his word about being a better man to me.

"Oh my God! What is he doing here?" I said to myself in a panic.

When I was pulling up to the house, Rico was in the driveway. I almost shit in my pants. I couldn't deal with him right now, on top of everything else. That was the last thing I needed.

Instead of pulling in, I just kept driving past the house. I looked in my rearview to see if Rico had seen me. He didn't seem to react like he had seen me. Thank God for that.

I went to the store to buy a ginger ale to help with my constant nausea. I loitered around the store, wasting time in hopes that Rico would be gone by the time I drove back. I must have looked like a crack addict the way I was pacing up and down the aisles. I just couldn't stay still, I was so worked up and on edge. Everything was happening too fast.

I tried to read a magazine, but it was impossible for me to concentrate on any of it. I threw the magazine down and went back to my car. If Rico was there, so be it. I had dealt with enough shit today. What's one more little drama?

"Whew!" I gave a sigh of relief as I drove up.

Rico's car was out of the driveway. He had left. I pulled in the driveway and waited for Touch. I sat singing along to the tunes of Keri Hilson, desperately trying to keep my mind off my problems. As I sat there, through my rearview mirror, I got a glimpse of Touch pulling up. He parked on the street in front of the house instead of coming into the driveway.

He must be angry with me, I thought.

As I was opening my car door, I saw Rico rush toward Touch from next door. That's when I realized he hadn't left. He'd just parked his car someplace else. I jumped out of the car and headed in their direction, but before I could reach them, Rico and Touch had already locked eyes, and both pulled out their guns.

"No!" I yelled, as I ran to get between them.

As soon as I reached them, shots were fired. I looked down to see my white shirt turn dark red. Realizing I'd been shot, I grabbed my stomach.

"My baby!" I yelled, collapsing on the ground. Looking up from the ground, I saw Touch come running over to me.

He threw himself on the ground next to me and cradled my head. "Bae, you okay?" he screamed. "Stay with me!"

I was starting to have trouble breathing. I felt like I was going in and out of consciousness. I tried to speak, but I could only moan as blood trickled from my mouth.

Touch was crying and rocking me back and forth like a baby. "Jewel, don't give up. I love you. I'm sorry for everything."

I looked into his eyes, and in the faintest whisper, I was able to say, "Baby."

He looked at me surprised. "Did you say *baby*?"

I nodded my head slowly, every movement for me painful at that point.

"Are you pregnant?" he asked.

I nodded again.

"Is it mine?"

I nodded yet again and smiled.

I heard Touch say one last time, "I love you."

And the darkness slowly came to my eyes. I couldn't fight anymore, but I was happy to know that Touch truly loved me.

ORDER FORM
URBAN BOOKS, LLC
78 E. Industry Ct
Deer Park, NY 11729

Name: (please print):_____

Address: _____

City/State: _____

Zip: _____

QTY	TITLES	PRICE

Shipping and handling-add $3.50 for 1st book, then $1.75 for each additional book.

Please send a check payable to:

Urban Books, LLC

Please allow 4-6 weeks for delivery

ORDER FORM
URBAN BOOKS, LLC
78 E. Industry Ct
Deer Park, NY 11729

Name: (please print):_____

Address: _____

City/State: _____

Zip: _____

QTY	TITLES	PRICE
	16 On The Block	$14.95
	A Girl From Flint	$14.95
	A Pimp's Life	$14.95
	Baltimore Chronicles	$14.95
	Baltimore Chronicles 2	$14.95
	Betrayal	$14.95
	Black Diamond	$14.95
	Black Diamond 2	$14.95
	Black Friday	$14.95
	Both Sides Of The Fence	$14.95
	Both Sides Of The Fence 2	$14.95
	California Connection	$14.95

Shipping and handling-add $3.50 for 1st book, then $1.75 for each additional book.

Please send a check payable to:

Urban Books, LLC

Please allow 4-6 weeks for delivery

ORDER FORM
URBAN BOOKS, LLC
78 E. Industry Ct
Deer Park, NY 11729

Name: (please print): _____

Address: _____

City/State: _____

Zip: _____

QTY	TITLES	PRICE
	California Connection 2	$14.95
	Cheesecake And Teardrops	$14.95
	Congratulations	$14.95
	Crazy In Love	$14.95
	Cyber Case	$14.95
	Denim Diaries	$14.95
	Diary Of A Mad First Lady	$14.95
	Diary Of A Stalker	$14.95
	Diary Of A Street Diva	$14.95
	Diary Of A Young Girl	$14.95
	Dirty Money	$14.95
	Dirty To The Grave	$14.95

Shipping and handling-add $3.50 for 1st book, then $1.75 for each additional book.

Please send a check payable to:
  Urban Books, LLC
Please allow 4-6 weeks for delivery

ORDER FORM
URBAN BOOKS, LLC
78 E. Industry Ct
Deer Park, NY 11729

Name: (please print):_____

Address: _____

City/State: _____

Zip: _____

QTY	TITLES	PRICE
	Gunz And Roses	$14.95
	Happily Ever Now	$14.95
	Hell Has No Fury	$14.95
	Hush	$14.95
	If It Isn't love	$14.95
	Kiss Kiss Bang Bang	$14.95
	Last Breath	$14.95
	Little Black Girl Lost	$14.95
	Little Black Girl Lost 2	$14.95
	Little Black Girl Lost 3	$14.95
	Little Black Girl Lost 4	$14.95
	Little Black Girl Lost 5	$14.95

Shipping and handling-add $3.50 for 1st book, then $1.75 for each additional book.

Please send a check payable to:

Urban Books, LLC

Please allow 4-6 weeks for delivery